# THE SIEGE OF DRAGONSBANE KEEP
### and
### Other Tales from Drascara

by

Roger Stockman & Daniel E. Myers

This book is dedicated to my core group of friends who brought the characters in The Siege of Dragonsbane Keep to life: Dan Myers, Erik Olsrud, Jerry Prindle, and Rick Trierweiler. I could not have written the novella without your portrayals of these characters. I may have made many changes to the adventure, but I hope I have kept the spirit of it.

Foreword

I want to take some time to thank some individuals who helped me make this book a reality. First of all, thank you to everyone holding this book and reading it. It is much appreciated, and I hope you enjoy the stories in this anthology.

I have been an avid reader of fantasy since my middle school years. Many fantasy authors have fueled my imagination for my writing. The following authors have been most instrumental in my development as a writer: J.R.R. Tolkien, David Eddings, Raymond E. Feist, Robert Jordan, and Brandon Sanderson. I would like to thank these authors for being such master storytellers. You have truly been an inspiration to me.

I would also like to thank my editor, Beth Rodgers. Beth has served as an editor on multiple projects of mine, and I always appreciate her dedication and insightfulness.

I want to thank my wife, Ayumi, who has always given me great support in my writing ambitions. She has had to put up with me sequestering myself for whole weekends in order for me get words on the page.

Finally, I would like to thank my long-time great friend, Dan Myers, who has invited me into his fantasy world and allowed me to create stories with him.

# CONTENTS

# THE SIEGE OF DRAGONSBANE KEEP
by
Roger Stockman

Year 576, AOE (Age of the elementalists)

*Dragonsbane Keep was situated on the Great Forest's northwestern border. Founded five years earlier by adventurers on the ruins of an abandoned Forest Spirit temple, Dragonsbane Keep was unusual because it was partly established by fire warriors in the Great Forest, the Great Aelf's home. For centuries, aelf and elementalists were bitter rivals, their uneasy peace holding only as long as the elementalists remained in the Drascara plains, avoiding the forests. The establishment of Dragonsbane Keep threatened to upset that balance. The party of Dragonsbane itself was an anomaly, consisting of two fire warriors, two half-aelf, one of which was a Forest Spirit priest, and an aelf mage, who herself was the daughter of the High Aelf king. It may have been her presence that prevented the residents of the Great Forest, the Great Aelf and the High Aelf, from destroying Dragonsbane Keep as it was being established.*

*The party of Dragonsbane established itself as a powerful group of adventurers. Its name actually came from its habit of hunting dragons in Drascara, slaying them, and taking their treasures. As adventurers, they were a motley crew who were often the subject of double-takes in the places they visited. A group with two fire warriors, two half-aelf, and a High Aelf was quite an unexpected sight. The company symbolized, for some, a world where diverse individuals could work together toward a common goal. Others considered it an abomination. After years of adventuring, the party semi-retired, using the treasures they had garnered over their time together to establish Dragonsbane Keep. They hoped to create a future freehold where all races could live harmoniously. Five years of harmony at Dragonsbane Keep ended with the arrival of strange beings from the north.*

৯৽৶

For five years, Dragonsbane Keep had been under construction. In that time, an area roughly three hundred yards square had been cleared of the large, ancient oak trees that had stood there for centuries. The trees had, in turn, been used for construction of the keep. In the center of the clearing, the walls of the keep, roughly one hundred yards to a side, had been constructed out of the rough-hewn timbers. The walls enclosed an ancient, abandoned Forest Spirit temple. On the south wall of the keep, a large wooden gate with iron reinforcements was placed at the center of the wall. Smaller, sally port-type doors were built into the other three walls. Construction of other inner buildings began after the completion of the wall. In addition to a five-foot wide catwalk on the north and south walls, a stables, an inn, and some barracks had been constructed inside the wall. Besides the various workmen needed to build the keep, the party of Dragonsbane had acquired quite a following: twenty fire mages, twenty Forest Spirit priests, and one thousand common soldiers. Apart from the occasional grendlaar incursions into their territory, Dragonsbane Keep had, for the most part, remained unmolested. That was until a large contingent of unknown forces appeared from the north.

Towering dark figures stood in formations surrounding Dragonsbane Keep. No one knew who or even what they were. These strange, eight-foot-tall creatures with hard, chitinous, grayish bodies, four arms and two legs, had suddenly appeared marching from the north through the Pine Woods until reaching their destination in the Great Forest. They wore no clothes, and their chests arched out to a thin edge in the center, which would render any slashing sword blows completely ineffective. Their hairless heads were something that would keep children awake at night. Covering half of the surface in what would be called the face on a human were two large, black, ovular and slightly raised discs. At the bottom of the face was a long fissure. When this fissure was opened wide, two rows of long, sharp teeth could be seen on the top and bottom. The dolmaari didn't appear to have any noses or ears, but two long strands, which could only be thought of as antennae, stuck out from the top of their heads. The dolmaari carried no weapons that anyone could see. No one had ever seen such creatures before. What was their purpose? Messengers had been sent out to parley with them, but they spoke a strange chittering language. Even with the help of magic spells, the only thing that could be deciphered from their strange language was that they were called dolmaari.

The dolmaari army had had Dragonsbane Keep under siege for ten full days now. Del Nilippez Pyrodeus was just finishing an inspection tour of his defenses. "Hey, you on the wall there!" Del barked at a soldier who was casually leaning up against the rampart. "Stay alert!"

"Stay alive!" the soldier called back in the ritualistic style that was customary in Del's army as he snapped to attention.

Del turned to the man next to him. "Korjinn, take command of the watch. I have to go to a strategy meeting at the temple."

"Yes, sir!" Korjinn said with a salute. He ran off, bellowing something at one of the soldiers as he went.

Del started toward the temple. Dragonsbane Keep didn't have a proper manor house yet, so an ancient Forest Spirit temple had to be used for the command post. He supposed the others were already waiting for him there. Del hoped Drake would give the order to initiate the counterattack on the dolmaari forces. Del hated this waiting game. As he approached the front door, he noticed some temple priests busily attending the gardens. It amazed Del that they could be engaging in such a mundane activity when an attack was imminent. He entered the temple into the main hall and steered toward the door on the left-hand wall that led into the conference room.

As he entered, he saw the others already seated at the table, waiting for him. Drake Pyronius was seated at the head of the table. Drake and Del, with their square-jawed faces and dark eyes, looked like they could have been twins, when in reality they were cousins. However, until just a few years earlier, people would have difficulty telling them apart if it weren't for Del's jet-black hair and Drake's dark auburn hair. Now, however, the scar running down the left side of Del's face from his temple to his jaw also made it impossible to mistake one for the other. To Drake's left, on the side of the table, was Elian Revilasi, Dragonsbane Keep's Forest Spirit priest. Elian's slightly pointed ears emerging through his light brown hair betrayed the fact that he was half-aelf. Next to Elian was Lady Silvervale, a radiant High Aelf princess with flowing silver hair. Del headed to the empty chair across from Elian. He walked past Zevirilyn, a slight, fidgety man with unkempt bright-red hair and a red handlebar moustache that was in a constant state of twitching. Del sat down next to Laarandolthanus, a half-aelf with blond hair and faintly pointed ears. Everyone, except Silvervale, called him Laaran.

"Good. We can get started now," Drake said. "Is everyone ready to give their reports?"

Before anyone could reply, Del jumped out of his chair, slammed his gauntleted fist against the table, and shouted, "We need to attack now!" The entire table shook violently under the tremendous force. "We can't last much longer just hiding inside this prison." Del began pacing as he went on his tirade. "We'll starve to death eventually!"

Drake tried to calm Del down. "We all know this, Del. So I've been thinking about a course of action, but I need to hear the reports before making any decisions."

"Think! Think!" Del started pacing. "That's all you ever do is think! But we need action now, not thinking!" Del thrust an armored index finger at Drake.

Drake's anger revealed itself with a flash from his amber eyes. He stood as he said, "Everyone, including you, put me in my position precisely because I think before I act!"

"You're right, Del," Elian interjected to stave off a possible physical confrontation. "But we need to think first and then act. It won't do anybody any good if we go off and act rashly without considering all the options. So please sit down, Del."

Del reluctantly took his seat. There were times when only Elian could calm Del down. Del had great respect for the Forest Spirit priest.

"Can we get to the reports now, Del?" Drake asked. Del nodded agreement. "Good." Drake turned to Elian. "Elian, what do you have to report?"

"Unfortunately, I have received no guidance from the Forest Spirits on this matter yet. This isn't unusual, unfortunately. I can usually only commune with them at an active Forest Spirit temple. I'm afraid we'll have to rely on our own judgment. However, my priests will soon be ready for casualties. We will have a triage area set up in front of the temple where we can administer treatment; and Dragonsbane Inn has been converted into a hospital ward."

"Well, that part is good, at least." Drake turned to Del. "Are our forces ready to attack?"

"As ready as they'll ever be," Del answered.

"What are our numbers like?"

"We have about one thousand able-bodied, fighting men in our own forces. Of course, we'll have to keep about one hundred of those in the keep as a defensive force. We also have the honor guard of the Dwarven Envoy. They number about one hundred. It was really fortunate they were here at this time."

"I'll be sure to tell them how fortunate you think it is," commented Laaran.

Del ignored the comment. He didn't much appreciate Laaran's wry wit in the best of times, which these certainly weren't. "And we also have a new addition to our forces." Everyone snapped to attention and stared at Del. Del, appreciating the suspense of the moment, didn't immediately offer any further information.

"Well, are you going to tell us?" asked Zevirilyn.

Del made a wide grin as he leaned back in his chair and clasped his hands behind his head. "No, I'm quite enjoying this. I'll think I'll wait awhile."

"Del—" Drake began sternly.

Del motioned for Drake to stop. "No, no, I'll finish. You have no sense of humor, Drake. About one hour ago, one hundred grendlaar archers arrived from the grackle chieftain. They were able to sneak through the dolmaari encampment. It was lucky I was at that part of the keep when they came. Our guards were ready to fire upon them."

"They came to *help* us?" Silvervale asked. "We cannot accept their help. They are—"

"Evil," Del completed Silvervale's statement. "Yes, we know, Silvervale, but I don't think we can afford to turn them away."

"I think we need a vote of the council," said Drake.

"I'll leave while you vote," offered Zevirilyn.

"That won't be necessary, Zevirilyn," said Drake. "We can finish this quickly. What do you say, Del? Accept the grendlaar help—yes or no?"

"Yes, yes! Definitely, yes!"

"Elian?"

"No, I'm sorry, but I'm going to have to agree with Silvervale on this one. We can't trust the grendlaar. They may just shoot their bows into the keep at us."

"Fair enough. Silvervale?"

"No! Definitely, no! We cannot accept alliances with those demons!"

Del rolled his eyes. "Leave it to you to overdramatize the situation, Silvervale." Silvervale shot Del an indignant look.

"Laaran?" Drake queried for the final vote.

"Yes. I have no qualms about accepting their help. Who knows? They might accidentally stick an arrow into a non-vital part of Del. It could dramatically improve his disposition."

Del made a disgusted face at this comment, and then turned to Drake. "That makes it two to two, which means you have to decide, Drake."

"Yes, I know." Drake paused for a moment. "Alright, here is my decision. We will accept their help, but we will leave an additional one hundred soldiers. These extra hundred soldiers will be assigned to watch the grendlaar. One man for each grendlaar. That should allay Elian's fears. I'm sorry, but I can't do anything about your conscience, Silvervale."

"But it doesn't make any sense," erupted Del. "It's just trading one hundred soldiers for a different hundred soldiers."

"Correct me if I'm wrong, Del, but I think one hundred grendlaar archers are a greater asset than one hundred of our own ground troops. We've been on the receiving end of those archers before; you know how good they are," countered Drake.

"Well, I suppose that's true," conceded Del.

"I can live with this compromise," said Elian.

"I do not think I can; however, I am willing to abide by the decision of the group," said Silvervale.

"Good. Now we can continue with the reports. Are you finished, Del?"

"Yes, except for the battle plan, which I will explain after I hear all the reports."

"Fine. Silvervale?"

"Yes. My mages are ready to assume their positions on the wall, armed with the scrolls we have been writing for the past week. I think the same can be said for the fire mages. Is that not correct, Zevirilyn?"

"Yes. My fire mages are ready for the attack."

"Excellent. What do you have to report, Laaran?"

"The intelligence reports I've received are a little discouraging. It appears the size of the dolmaari is much larger than we first suspected. It appears they number about ten thousand." Everyone gasped at the figure. "They surround the keep at a distance of about one hundred yards, staying mostly in the tree line. However, there is no evidence of dolmaari reinforcements from any direction, so I think ten thousand is their entire force."

"Isn't that enough?" exploded Elian. "This counter attack cannot succeed! Their force is too great!"

"I can decide on whether to proceed with a counterattack after we hear Del's battle plan," said Drake. "Please continue, Laaran."

"Thank you. Furthermore, our reports indicate that the greatest concentration of their force is mustered to the south of the keep outside our front gate." Laaran pointed out this position on the map, which was spread out on the conference table in front of them. "They have about four thousand there. The second greatest force is to the north, about here." Laaran indicated the position to the northwest of the keep. "They have about three thousand soldiers there. The remaining forces are spread pretty evenly around the keep to the east and west. It doesn't appear as if they are readying an attack, so they may be trying to starve us out."

"We'll have to make sure that doesn't happen. We can take the fight to them and break this siege!" erupted Del.

"How can we do that, Del? We don't have enough forces to take on ten thousand dolmaari," countered Elian.

"I believe I may have a solution that will somewhat even the odds," interjected Silvervale.

"Let's hear it," Drake said.

"If I can get to my father in the Great Forest, I may be able to return with a few branches of aelf cavalry, maybe even a whole trunk."

"That certainly would turn the odds in our favor," Del acknowledged.

"Why would your father help us, though?" Drake countered. "We all know how he feels about us building our keep at the edge of the Great Forest. Refusing aid could be a way for him to rid the aelf of our presence here," Drake countered.

"I believe my father will not be able to resist the charms of his only daughter. Besides, even my father should be able to see that the dolmaari threat is greater than any threat we pose."

"How will you get through the dolmaari lines, though?" inquired Elian.

"I can make sure she gets through safely," Laaran offered. "We can leave about two hours before first light. I can escort her to the other side and return before any attack begins."

"What will be the plan when Silvervale returns with the High Aelf cavalry?" Del asked.

"I suppose it will depend on how many cavalry troops Silvervale returns with. If she returns with a sizable force, we could perform a clamp maneuver and crush the dolmaari between the keep's forces and the High Aelf cavalry. If the force is smaller, we could get them inside the keep to add to our forces," Drake answered. "Silvervale, is there a way for you to send us a message once you've arrived back at the keep with the cavalry?"

"Yes, I can successfully send a message to Elian once I have arrived."

Drake pinched his lips together, thrust them out, and nodded his head up and down repeatedly as he always did when he was thinking intently about something. "Are you finished with your report, Laaran?"

"I have one more thing. On one of my scouting missions, I think I may have learned a weakness in the anatomy of the dolmaari. It appears they may have a groove at the base of their skulls. One could probably slip a dagger in there for a killing blow. Of course, you'd have to be quiet and quick enough to get behind them and stab at precisely the right spot to deliver this lethal blow. I haven't had a chance to test it yet, but I'm sure I could manage it if I can get close enough. And that's it. That's all from me, unless you want to hear what they are using to wipe their—"

"Laarandolthanus!" exclaimed Silvervale. Laaran smirked at having gotten a reaction out of Silvervale.

Del turned to Drake. "Have you heard from the Elemental Palace of Fire concerning our request for aid?"

"No, Garaz hasn't sent a messenger ahead of the force of one hundred fire warriors we sent him to retrieve. So, we are going to have to rely on the forces currently here in the keep. In light of the fact that the dolmaari force is much larger than first believed and Silvervale's upcoming mission, I believe it would be prudent to delay any attack until Silvervale returns."

Del shot out of his seat once more, his face now a bright red. "No! We need to attack now!"

Drake stood up quickly. "I've made my decision, Del," he said with barely controlled rage, his amber eyes flashing in anger. "The dolmaari haven't shown any signs of an imminent attack. With the addition of aelf cavalry, our odds of victory significantly increase. Delaying an attack for a couple of days won't adversely affect us. Surely, you can see this, Del."

Del looked as if he was about to explode again, when Elian stood up and addressed Del soothingly. "Del, Drake's plan has wisdom. We should listen to what he has to say." Elian walked up to Del and placed a calming hand on Del's shoulder.

"Oh, very well," Del responded as he took his seat and Elian returned to his.

"Del, we can spend the next few days training our new recruits," said Drake. Del nodded his agreement. "Very well, you are all dismissed."

৽৽৶

A few hours later, Laaran and Silvervale slipped through the sally port located in the eastern wall of Dragonsbane Keep. Off in the distance, they could see fires burning.

"This way," whispered Laaran as he moved off in a southeasterly direction. Silvervale stayed on his heels. They had moved maybe a hundred yards to the southeast when Laaran turned to Silvervale. "Wait here." Silvervale stopped as Laaran disappeared into the darkness.

Silvervale could hear a stifled yelp from the direction Laaran had gone. She continued to wait for several minutes, but Laaran still had not returned. "Laaran," she whispered into the blackness. "Laaran."

Silvervale gasped as someone grabbed her from behind and put a hand over her mouth. "Shh!" Laaran scolded. "Do you want to bring the whole army down on us?"

"What took you so long?"

"I found a sentry," Laaran answered. "I dispatched him without much difficulty, but I was unable to stop him from making a sound. The noise attracted the attention of a few more sentries. We'll have to change direction."

Laaran took Silvervale's hand and pulled her off to the northwest. "Laaran, we are going the wrong way," Silvervale said.

"Yes, I know, but do you want to get to your father in one piece? You'll be no use to anyone dead." Laaran continued to lead Silvervale through the forest and then turned straight north. After about ten minutes of walking north, Laaran abruptly veered to the southeast again. When they were about fifty yards inside the tree line, he came to an unexpected halt. He placed two fingers in his mouth and made a whistling sound not unlike one of a black nut bird.

After a minute or so, Silvervale could see movement coming toward them. She made a move to hide behind a tree, but Laaran stopped her. "Relax, this is my boy, Dickie." Silvervale could then see the outline of a small boy leading a horse. It looked to be a thoroughbred, but she couldn't exactly tell in the darkness. "Okay," Laaran continued. "We're through the dolmaari lines, but they could still have roving sentries around here. Get on the horse and ride straight east for three hursmarcs. By then you should be past any patrols. Then you can head straight for your home. Do you think you can find your way alright?"

Silvervale cast a disdainful look at Laaran. "I have lived in this forest for my entire life. Of course, I can find my way." Silvervale mounted the horse bareback and headed off to the east at a light gallop. Laaran and Dickie headed back in the direction of Dragonsbane Keep.

৽৽

The next morning, Del and Drake stood in front of their one hundred new recruits in the open area between the front gate and the temple. They had been training them for the past four weeks. Fortunately, they had arrived before the dolmaari suddenly appeared around Dragonsbane Keep. Four weeks wasn't enough time for them to make them competent infantrymen, so they would be replacing guardsmen on the wall. In turn, those guardsmen would be incorporated into the infantry. They now had only a few more days to train them.

Since the new recruits would be used to defend the wall, they were primarily trained in the use of pikes in order to prevent the dolmaari from getting into the keep over the walls. Their training included a lot of repetitive drills of thrusting downward with pikes from atop hogshead barrels. "Thrust!" shouted Del. The recruits drove their pikes forward and down. "Withdraw!" The recruits drew back their pikes. And so this went on and on.

"Del!" Elian called as he exited the temple.

Del turned his attention toward Elian. "Drake, take over training while I go to see what Elian wants." Drake nodded his assent, and Del started off toward Elian. Suddenly, Del was horrified by the appearance of a dolmaari directly behind Elian. The dolmaari appeared to rise directly out of the ground. "Elian, watch out!"

Elian turned around to see the dolmaari towering over him. Five claws shot out from the fingers of each of the four hands and began arcing toward Elian. There was no time for Elian to react. Del shot off at a sprint toward Elian. Del hadn't gone more than a few paces when he saw the dolmaari soldier fall face first to the ground, on top of Elian. Behind where the dolmaari soldier had been standing was Laaran, a bloodied short sword clenched in both hands. Laaran and Del immediately grabbed the dead body of the dolmaari and pulled it off of Elian.

Drake, seeing what was happening near the temple, broke into a sprint. Once arriving, he asked, "Elian, are you alright?"

"A little bruised, but I've had worse," he answered.

"How did that thing even get in the keep?" asked Del.

"That's something Laaran is going to have to find out," Drake answered.

Laaran, taking that as a command, trotted off in the direction from which the dolmaari soldier had come. "I'll let you know if I find any more of them lurking about," called Laaran as he trotted off.

"Del, have some soldiers do a sweep of the keep to find any other dolmaari that may have gotten inside," said Drake.

"Of course, Drake," responded Del as he headed toward the front gate.

℔ℕ

Laaran squatted on the ground and looked for signs of dolmaari tracks inside of the keep. He wasn't an expert tracker, but it shouldn't be too hard to retrace the huge footprints of the dolmaari soldier that had managed to get inside the keep. The dolmaari had definitely come into the keep from the west. However, he found the tracks to be odd. There were definite footprints; however, there also appeared to be handprints on the ground. He wondered if the dolmaari moved along the ground on all six limbs. He continued to follow the set of tracks. When he was about fifty feet from the wall, he detected that the one set of tracks suddenly became several. It was difficult to tell how many, but he guessed it was at least five. He continued his way up to the wall and found the sally port in the western wall was swinging freely. *That solves the mystery of how the dolmaari got in the keep,* he thought. *But how did they manage to get up to the wall without being seen?*

Laaran thought about his next course of action. He had to secure the sally port so that no more dolmaari could get inside the keep. Then he had to determine how many dolmaari managed to get inside the keep and figure out where they went. He retraced his way back to the spot where he first noticed there were several sets of footprints. From there he could see several sets of tracks heading off in different directions. After some investigation, he counted at least seven sets of tracks, including the original set that he had followed. This could be a problem.

He decided his first order of business would be to get the sally port secured. He immediately headed to Dragonsbane Inn. Once inside, he called for James, the chief engineer. A man came running down the steps from the second floor. "Yes, milord?"

"James, a small group of dolmaari has breached the sally port in the west wall." James blanched at Laaran's statement. "I need you to take a couple of laborers, some supplies, and tools to close the breach."

"B-b-but won't that be dangerous, milord?" James' voice wavered in fear.

"Yes, but it will be more dangerous not to close it. Don't worry. I'll have some soldiers sent to that location to protect you as you repair the damage."

"Very well, milord. I'll get on it right away." James ran back up the steps.

Laaran spun around, left the inn, and headed to the front gate. "Korjinn!" he called when he got there.

A head peeked over the battlement. "Yes, Lord Laaran?" queried Korjinn.

"Can you come down here for a moment?"

"Yes, milord," Korjinn replied and began his descent down the spiral staircase. "What is it, milord?" he asked when he reached the bottom of the staircase.

"The dolmaari have breached the sally port in the western wall," Laaran explained.

"How did that happen, milord?" Korjinn asked.

"I'm not sure, but in that area of the wall, we don't have a catwalk on the parapet. That's why they must have been able to sneak in there."

"How many are there, milord?"

"It's a small force, probably no more than ten, but they could present some problems inside the walls. Therefore, I need you to send one squad of soldiers to that sally port to protect the laborers as they repair the breach. I also need you to send two squads of soldiers to do a sweep of the interior of the keep to locate and dispatch those dolmaari infiltrators."

"I already have soldiers sweeping the keep. Lord Del gave the order a few minutes ago, but I'll dispatch soldiers to the western wall immediately. Korjinn started growling commands to a sergeant on the wall.

Laaran then headed back to the western wall to follow tracks to the remaining dolmaari infiltrators. When he arrived at the wall, James and the laborers were already there. "Excellent, James!" Laaran complimented. "You got here quickly. I'll see to it that you and your men get a bonus for this."

"Thank you, milord!" cried the chorus of laborers.

"I'll stay here to protect you until the soldiers get here." Laaran only had to wait a few minutes until the soldiers arrived. Then he looked for where the other tracks led to. It appeared at least two dolmaari had headed off in the direction of the stables, so Laaran followed the tracks there.

When Laaran arrived at the stables, he could see the wide door slightly ajar. He approached the door quietly and managed to slip inside. The nervous braying of horses could be heard. He hid in the darkness near the door and listened intently. He could hear voices coming from the far side of the stables. It was the harsh, chittering language of the dolmaari. Laaran continued to move silently along the wall to get closer to the voices. He could see bright sparks flashing in the darkness. Laaran managed to get within five feet of two dolmaari without being detected. Gripping his short sword in his right hand, he leapt from the shadows and thrust his blade into the base of the skull of the dolmaari nearest him, using the strength of both arms. The dolmaari crumpled to the ground. The other dolmaari cried out in shock, but it made no defensive move. He simply looked behind Laaran.

When Laaran was just about to look behind him, he felt something hard smash against the back of his skull. And then everything went black.

ço∽ɹ

It took Silvervale nearly three hours of hard riding to reach the edge of her father's kingdom. Since this forest was her home, she had little difficulty navigating her way. The High Aelf also kept the area clear of any threats. Once Silvervale crossed into her kingdom, she slowed her ride to a comfortable trot. She was almost immediately met by several cloaked figures who suddenly appeared out of the landscape ahead of her.

"Beannachtaí, Whitesky!" Silvervale said, greeting one of the figures.

The figure cast off the hood of his cloak to reveal white hair and sharp aelf features. "Banphrionsa! Thank the Forest Spirits we have found you. Your father sent us to look for you because of the strange creatures lurking in our forest," replied Whitesky.

"I was just on my way to see him."

"We will take you to him immediately. He anxiously awaits news of your well-being," said Whitesky. The other aelf gathered horses that seemed to materialize out of the aether.

Whitesky mounted the steed brought to him. "Do you think it was wise, Banphrionsa, to travel alone with those creatures roaming in the forest?"

"Do you mean the dolmaari?"

"Is that what they are called, Your Highness?" asked Whitesky.

"They are the reason I have come. They have Dragonsbane Keep under siege. I am coming to ask my father for aid."

"You should not get your hopes up for help from your father," Whitesky added. "You know how he feels about your…" Whitesky paused to think of a word that would not offend his princess, "…companions."

"We shall see, Whitesky. We shall see. We should ride quickly. It is of great import that I return to Dragonsbane Keep as soon as possible." With that, Silvervale kicked her horse into a quick gallop. Her aelf escorts did the same.

It took nearly an hour of riding before they reached the palace of the High Aelf king.

All of the riders dismounted, and Silvervale approached the sentry at the gate. "Take me to my father at once!" Silvervale commanded.

"As you command, Banphrionsa!"

Silvervale turned back to Whitesky. "I thank you for the escort, Whitesky. I should go in alone."

"I am sorry, Banphrionsa, but your father commanded me to bring you to him personally."

Silvervale sighed her acquiescence. "Very well, lead on." Silvervale gestured for Whitesky to go ahead of her. The sentries opened the gates of the palace, and Silvervale and Whitesky entered. As soon as they entered the palace, an aelf boy jumped to his feet from the stool on which he had been sitting "Boy! Go tell the High King that the Banphrionsa will meet him in the Great Hall," instructed Whitesky. Without saying a word, the boy bolted off and was soon out of sight. Silvervale and Whitesky proceeded across the entry hall to the double doors that led to the Great Hall.

"Do you remember, Báníon, when we ran through these halls together as children?" Silvervale asked, referring to Whitesky by his aelf nickname.

"Remember, Your Highness? It is my fondest memory."

Silvervale shook her head in a mock-scolding manner. "Please, Bánion. We are alone now. You may call me by my name."

"As you command, Silvervale," replied Whitesky.

A sad look came over Silvervale's face. "It is not a command, Bánion." After a moment, Silvervale continued, "What happened to us, Bánion? We used to be so close. We could tell each other anything. We had no secrets."

"We grew up, Silvervale," Whitesky replied matter-of-factly. Silvervale sighed at the simple truth.

When they arrived at the doors to the Great Hall, Whitesky opened the left door and gestured for Silvervale to enter. Whitesky entered the Great Hall behind Silvervale. They were both surprised to see the High King already sitting on his throne. He was flanked by a pair of soldiers, standing nearby "Mo iníon grá!" the High King exclaimed as he leapt off his throne and bounded toward Silvervale. He embraced her. "My beloved daughter! It is magnificent to see you home safe and sound!"

"Thank you, Father," Silvervale replied meekly.

"I was so afraid for you out in the forest with those creatures all around."

"They are called dolmaari, Father. They are the reason I have come to speak with you."

"Now, now," the High King continued in a fatherly tone, "there is no need to be so hasty. You will need a good night's rest and a hot bath. I will have you escorted to your chambers. We can talk later in the morning. We must have a great feast tomorrow to honor your return."

"But, Father, I am afraid I really do not have the time. I must return to Dragonsbane Keep as soon as I am able."

The High King's face darkened briefly at the mention of Dragonsbane Keep. "Please, daughter, we can talk in the morning. Go get some rest." The High King gestured for the guards at the throne to come forward. "Lord Blue-tree, see the Banphrionsa safely to her quarters."

"Yes, Your Majesty," Lord Bluetree replied. He directed his attention to Silvervale. "After you, Banphrionsa." Silvervale began walking to the doors to the Great Hall ahead of Lord Bluetree and the other soldier, leaving her father and Whitesky behind her. Her frustration was palpable in the air.

༄

Laaran awoke as he was being carried over the shoulder by someone. He was bound and gagged with a hood over his head. He couldn't tell where he was. He didn't smell horse manure, so he guessed he was no longer in the stables. He wondered if he was still in Dragonsbane Keep. He felt himself being lowered to the ground. He thought that it shouldn't be too much trouble to free himself from his bonds if they would leave him alone for a few moments.

Laaran removed the hood from his head and looked in the direction of the chittering voices. He could see two dolmaari moving away from him. His eyes must have been playing tricks, because as he continued to look off in their direction, they seemed to blend into the darkness and almost disappear. However, he could hear their guttural voices fading. Now was his chance to get loose before they returned. Laaran took advantage of his flexibility to bend his body in an awkward fashion to recover a knife that was secreted into a slot in his left boot. He deftly flipped the blade into his right hand and began cutting the rope that bound his wrists together. Once his hands were free, he immediately removed the hood from his head. He quickly looked around. The keep was still in sight, and if he had his bearings straight, he thought it looked to be about a hundred yards to the southeast. He looked off in the other directions and could see two dolmaari soldiers about thirty yards to the northwest. In the distance, he could see the campfires of the main dolmaari encampment. Just a few hours earlier, he had escorted Silvervale through this part of the forest. Laaran set to work to cut the bindings at his ankles so that he could move. Once free, he quickly hid behind a tree and looked to the two dolmaari. They still had not looked back, and therefore had not noticed how he had freed himself.

Laaran briefly considered killing his two dolmaari captors before returning to the keep but decided that discretion was the better part of valor. He darted back toward the keep, moving swiftly and silently, while still trying to stay out of sight of his abductors. After making it back to the keep easily enough, he could hear a great uproar from inside. He slipped in through the sally port and secured it behind him. He had to quickly locate Drake. He figured that shouldn't be too difficult because he could immediately see flames high in the air from the area near the stables. Drake would most likely be there to combat the fire.

As Laaran moved off in the direction of the stables, he stumbled across two more dolmaari as he rounded the corner of one of the soldiers' barracks. They seemed more surprised than he was to see him appear so suddenly. They recovered quickly, however, and one of them shot the blade-like claws from all four hands and swiped them toward Laaran, who tumbled to the rear to avoid the strikes. *Curses!* he thought to himself. *I only have this knife to defend myself.* He somersaulted behind the dolmaari that had tried to strike him. He thrust the tip of the knife into the calf of the dolmaari, who cried out in pain as he fell to his knees. Laaran quickly withdrew the blade and planted it into the base of the dolmaari's skull. Laaran placed his right boot onto the back of the dolmaari and kicked him free. The dolmaari fell face-first into the hard ground with a dull thud. The other dolmaari tried to grab at Laaran and managed to punch him hard in the left shoulder. Laaran winced in pain. He thought the blow may have dislocated his shoulder. Being that he was probably in no condition now to fight this dolmaari one-on-one, Laaran took advantage of his speed and sprinted off toward the stables.

The dolmaari pursued Laaran but immediately broke off pursuit when they came within sight of four soldiers who were on patrol. Laaran called to them, "There's a dolmaari off in that direction." He pointed in the direction from where he had come.

"Yes, Lord Laaran! We'll take care of him," one of them shouted back. The soldiers darted past Laaran as he continued toward the stables.

Laaran finally arrived at the stables and was able to spot Drake immediately calling out orders to the trainees who were pitching buckets of water on the fire. Laaran dashed up to Drake.

"Ah, there you are, Laaran. We were wondering where you had gotten off to," said Drake.

Laaran shrugged. "A minor setback. I see you have the fire nearly under control." He looked at the guards and recruits forming lines to pass buckets of water to the front to douse the fire. "Were any of the horses killed?"

"Fortunately, no. We arrived in time to get them out before the fire got too out of hand. Have you found any more dolmaari inside the keep?" inquired Drake.

Laaran briefly reported his experiences since finding the open sally port in the western wall. "I'm not sure if we've accounted for all of them yet," continued Laaran. "I'll continue the search now."

"No, Laaran. You appear to have sustained some injuries. Report to Elian at the temple to see about some healing." Laaran nodded and darted off to the temple.

Seeing the fire in the stables well in hand, Drake headed back toward the front gate to check in with Del.

"What's happening?" asked Del.

"It seems there were more dolmaari infiltrators. One group of them managed to set fire to the stables. The fire is well in hand."

"How much longer do you think we can hold up in here?" asked a frustrated Del.

"Hopefully, long enough for Silvervale to get back with reinforcements." Del let out an irritated growl.

⊱⊰

Silvervale spent most of the night pacing in her chambers. How was she supposed to sleep when her friends were beginning what would seem to be an unwinnable battle? Fatigue finally overtook her, so she sat in the chair to rest but found herself still unable to sleep. At last she heard a sharp rap on her door. She arose and moved to the door. She opened it to see Whitesky.

Whitesky took a few moments to look her up and down. "I see you did not get any sleep last night."

"Do I look that dreadful?" Silvervale asked.

"You could never look anything but beautiful," Whitesky responded.

Silvervale gave a slight smile at the compliment. "Is my father ready to see me now?"

"Yes, he is awaiting you in the Great Hall." Whitesky stepped aside and gestured with his right arm for Silvervale to precede him. Silvervale stepped out of her room, and Whitesky closed the door behind them. They walked side by side in silence through the residential hallways and down to the Great Hall.

When Silvervale entered the Great Hall, her father was sitting on his throne. "My daughter, did you not sleep at all last night?"

"Father, how can I sleep when my friends are in such danger?" Silvervale asked. The High King gave an almost imperceptible grimace at Silvervale's question. Not wanting to waste any more time, Silvervale charged straight into her request. "Father, I am here to formally request aid for Dragonsbane Keep. I respectfully ask that you send one trunk of cavalry with me to aid in the assault."

This time the High King gave a noticeable wince at such a bold request. "My beloved daughter," the High King responded, "even with all the love I bear you, surely, you can see that this is a most difficult request to honor. Dragonsbane Keep is an invader on sovereign aelf lands. To help them would be treasonous to our own kind. The Great King will be beyond furious if he discovered we gave any aid to the cursèd humans."

"I understand that, Father, and I know we will never see eye to eye when it comes to the humans. However, there is an even greater threat in the dolmaari who are currently invading the Great Forest. Dragonsbane Keep cannot stand against such a large force. Once it is overrun, how long will it be until they turn their attention to our own kingdom and to the Great King himself?"

The High King's face seemed to soften a little. "Yes, this is indeed something to consider. I may have to ponder this for a few days."

"But Father, Dragonsbane Keep may not be able to last a few more days!" pleaded Silvervale. She approached the High King. The guards on both sides of him moved to intercept, but the High King raised his right hand as a signal to them. The guards immediately returned to their positions. Silvervale continued to her father and knelt at his feet, taking his hands in hers. "Father, surely you must know I have nothing but the best interests of the aelf in mind when I make this request."

Silvervale's father sighed deeply as a smile arose from his face. "Mo iníon grá, you know I could never deny you anything. Perhaps there is some merit in what you say."

At that moment, a door opened on the side wall to the rear of the throne. Silvervale and her father looked toward the sound to see a tall, stately aelf woman with hawkish facial features stride into the throne room. Silvervale arose immediately and stood to her father's right to face the woman. The woman continued toward the pair of them until she faced Silvervale. "Airgeadglheann," she said in an icy voice.

"Dia dhuit, mháthair," Silvervale greeted back.

"What is this I hear about a request for aelf cavalry to defend the enemy of all aelf?" the queen demanded.

"As I was explaining to Father," Silvervale began, "the dolmaari pose a threat to all who inhabit the Great Forest, and possibly all of Drascara."

The High Queen returned an expressionless stare at Silvervale. Then she leaned over to the king's left ear and whispered.

The High King's face contorted into a grimace as the queen spoke to him. Silvervale's mother then stood and stared coldly at Silvervale.

The High King cleared his throat and said, "Perhaps it is a bit hasty to embroil the aelf in a battle between humans and these so-called dolmaari." The High King seemed to force these words out.

"But Father, as I said before, the dolmaari will most certainly turn their attention here after their inevitable victory over Dragonsbane Keep."

"We will have to confront that when we come to it. I am afraid I cannot grant your request." The High King's voice sounded almost sad as he spoke these words.

"Very well. Though I must say I am disappointed in you, Father. I will return to Dragonsbane Keep immediately." Just before Silvervale turned to leave, she saw her mother bend over and whisper into her father's ear once more.

Silvervale's father stood from his throne and said, "I am afraid I cannot allow that. It is far too dangerous for you to return to your friends. You should accept their fate and live in peace with your own kind from this day forward. Guards, take my daughter back to her chambers." Two guards stepped up to Silvervale, each grabbing one of her arms as they began to forcefully pull her from the Great Hall.

"Father!" Silvervale screamed. "Please, you must let me return!" The High King stood in silence as his daughter was forcibly removed from the Great Hall, her screams continuing to echo off the palace walls.

Silvervale fumed in her private quarters. How dare her father keep her prisoner here? She knew of his prejudice against humans and especially against the elementalists, but why could he not see that they were facing a common enemy? It was so frustrating. She was not a little girl anymore. She was old enough to make decisions for herself, yet her father insisted on "protecting" her still.

Silvervale heard a knock at her door. "Go away. I am not hungry."

"Silvervale?" she heard a familiar voice say from the other side.

"Whitesky? Is that you?"

"Yes, my lady."

Silvervale immediately opened the door and let Whitesky in. They embraced each other for a moment. Whitesky stepped back into the doorway and looked to either side. Then he closed the door behind him.

"Bánion, what are you doing here?"

"I have come to help you out of here."

Silvervale thought for a second, then shook her head. "I cannot allow you to do that, Bánion. My father will be furious with you. You may lose your command."

"I am willing to risk it. It is the right thing to do. The commanders of my Éodram branch have agreed to accompany you back to Dragonsbane Keep and assist you in any way we can."

"This is too much, Whitesky," Silvervale argued. "My father will never let you leave."

"Do I have to remind you, Princess, that the Éodram are light cavalry. Once we set off, we should easily be able to outdistance any pursuing cavalry."

"I know that, Whitesky, but I do not see how one hundred fifty units of light cavalry can make any significant impact on the outcome of the battle at Dragonsbane Keep."

"Let me ask you this. Do the odds of victory increase or decrease with the addition of one hundred fifty cavalry soldiers?"

"Well, increase, of course, but—"

"Then it is settled. Get your things together. I will return in one hour for you. Be ready by then." Silvervale nodded her acquiescence, and Whitesky slipped out the door.

Silvervale spent the next hour packing up her things. She also found several scrolls of magic spells which she had written before and left in her quarters months ago. She didn't have time to see what spells each individual scrolls contained, so she packed all of them. There had to be some powerful lightning spells in the lot.

True to his word, Whitesky returned in an hour. "Are you ready, Princess?" he asked. Silvervale nodded. The princess did not try to argue with him further. She knew it would get her nowhere. They slipped out the door, went to the right, and exited out of the royal palace through a servant's door. There were two horses waiting outside. One of them was Silvervale's.

"My branch is just to the west. We will meet them there." Silvervale nodded again.

Silvervale and Whitesky quickly mounted their horses and rode off toward the west. Within minutes of riding, Silvervale could see a large gathering of cavalry. Five mounted aelf approached Silvervale and Whitesky. "These are the captains of my leafs," Whitesky said.

"At your service, Your Highness," one of them said. The others uttered something similar.

"I cannot thank you enough for your help, Captaens. I only hope my father will show mercy to you upon your return," Silvervale offered.

"The king will come to see the wisdom of our decision in time, Princess," Whitesky interjected. Then he turned to his captains. "Let us mount up and move out."

"Yes, sir!" they all responded with a salute.

The captains rode off toward their individual leafs. The soldiers began mounting their warhorses. Soon they were riding off to the west toward Dragonsbane Keep.

Silvervale and Whitesky rode at the front of the Éodram branch of cavalry. After riding for a few hours, they were still several hours more from Dragonsbane Keep. Moving with a branch of cavalry through the forest proved to be quite a bit slower than traveling alone.

"Commander Whitesky! Princess Silvervale!" they heard a voice call from behind them. They stopped and turned their horses toward the voice. They saw a rider approaching them. When the rider reached them, he brought his horse to an abrupt halt.

"Yes, what is it, Redfern?" Whitesky inquired.

"A messenger has arrived from the king," answered Redfern.

Silvervale immediately blanched. "Oh, no!" she exclaimed. "I was afraid of this."

"Well, what does he have to say?" inquired Whitesky further.

"He would not say. He said he would only talk directly to the Banphrionsa."

"Well, bring him forward," commanded Silvervale.

"As you command, Your Majesty." Redfern turned his horse and gestured high in the air. Three riders rode up to them. Two of them stopped just shy of the group, and the third rode directly up to Silvervale.

"Well, what do you have to say for yourself?" Silvervale asked forcefully.

The messenger, looking nervous, cleared his throat and said, "Banphrionsa, the king has ordered you to return to the palace immediately and to bring back the Éodram leaf with you."

"Is that the full message?" Silvervale asked.

"Yes, Your Majesty."

"And this order was given directly to me?"

"Yes, Your Majesty."

"There was no order given for Whitesky?"

The messenger squirmed uncomfortably in his saddle. "No, Your Majesty," he finally admitted.

"Very well. Please return to the palace and inform my father that I respectfully decline to follow his command. My honor as a High Aelf princess prevents me from doing so." Silvervale took a second to concentrate on putting an authoritative tone in her voice. "You are dismissed."

The messenger immediately saluted Silvervale and said, "Yes, Banphrionsa!" Then he swung his horse around and galloped off in the direction of the palace.

"Do you think that was wise, my lady?" asked Whitesky. "The king will not be happy when he receives your response."

"I know, Whitesky, but I will deal with that when the time comes," replied Silvervale. "It was fortunate my father issued the order only to me. You do not have to worry about disobeying a direct order from the king. It will be all my responsibility. However, I will not hold you to your oath to me. You may return with your leaf if you feel that is the best course of action for you and your soldiers."

"I am, as always, at your command, my lady. I will not return unless you directly order me to."

"I will not do that, Whitesky. I will be glad to have your company and your assistance in the coming days."

"As you will, Banphrionsa," replied Whitesky. With that, Whitesky turned to his army and bellowed, "We ride in ten minutes! Be ready to ride hard the rest of the way!"

He was greeted with cries of, "Yes, sir!" and "For the honor of Whitesky!" and the like.


Princess Silvervale and Whitesky rode at the front of the branch of aelf cavalry well into the night with the tall black walnut trees of the forest towering above them.

"I would say we are about two hours from Dragonsbane Keep. Do you think we should stop for a rest or ride through?" asked Silvervale.

"Do not worry about my men, Íoncroí." Silvervale raised an eyebrow at Whitesky's use of her childhood nickname. She had not heard it used in many years. "They will be ready to fight either way."

"Then I suppose it would be best to get to the keep sooner rather than later."

They continued to ride through the night. Within two hours, just as the sun was beginning to peek above the eastern horizon, Silvervale could make out the smoke from the campfires of the dolmaari encampments. "Thank the Forest Spirits! They have not yet breached the walls."

"What are your orders, Banphrionsa?" asked Whitesky, reverting back to her courtly title.

"Tell your men to hold fast. I will contact Elian inside the keep. Perhaps they can cause a distraction and allow us to pass through the dolmaari lines and enter the keep."

"As you wish, Banphrionsa." Whitesky turned back to his captaens. "Ìoncaonach, Glastoir, coinnigh na línte," he said in a soft, yet commanding tone. The two aelf saluted Whitesky and rode off toward their leafs. Whitesky turned back to Silvervale and nodded.

Silvervale looked to the sky and blew out a discordant, high-pitched whistle. Within moments, a butterfly with large purple wings with yellow around the edges descended to her and landed on her right index finger. She whispered to the butterfly. The butterfly instantly flew off in the direction of the keep. The butterfly flitted high into the air and continued its journey. The butterfly flew high over eastern wall of Dragonsbane Keep and turned to the north.


Elian stood on the catwalk on the north side of the keep observing the dolmaari encampments in that direction. He suddenly noticed a purple butterfly alight on his shoulder. "What is it you want, little one?" Elian asked the winged insect as he tipped his ear in its direction and listened to what the creature had to tell him. Then Elian turned his head toward the butterfly and whispered to it. Within moments, the butterfly flew off. Elian turned to the interior of the keep and quickly spotted a messenger on the ground. "You, boy!" The messenger looked up at Elian. "Go find Lord Drake and tell him Lady

Silvervale has arrived. She is waiting at the edge of the tree line on the southeast side of the keep. They need an opening to get the aelf cavalry inside the keep."

"Yes, Lord Elian!" the messenger shouted as he ran off toward the center of the keep. As the messenger came around the southwest corner of Dragonsbane Inn, he immediately spotted Drake drilling soldiers in the open area. "Lord Drake!" he shouted as he ran up to him. "A message from Lord Elian. He says that Lady Silvervale has arrived with some aelf cavalry but needs you to create an opening so that they can safely enter the keep."

"Thank you, Hank. You may return to your post," Drake replied. The messenger darted back to where he had come from. "Del!" Drake shouted to his cousin.

Del looked over to his cousin and hurried over to him. "What is it, Drake?"

"Silvervale has arrived with the cavalry. We need to create an opening for them to get inside the keep."

Del let out a disappointed sigh. "That must mean she was only able to muster a small force. Well, we can add them to the numbers inside the walls. That should buy us a little time, at least. I'll get our ground troops ready."

"Very good," replied Drake. "I'll let Lord Darkstone know to muster up his dwarven infantry. Let's meet with our forces near the front gate in one hour."

Drake and Del ran off in separate directions to get ready for their foray into the dolmaari forces.

৵৵

Lady Silvervale waited atop her horse looking for the butterfly she had sent to Elian. She soon saw it returning. She held out a finger to allow the winged creature to land. Silvervale leaned her sharply pointed ear toward the butterfly. She then raised her head up and looked at Whitesky.

"Báníon," Silvervale called. "The time has come. Elian has sent me a message. They are going to create a diversion, so we will need an easy route inside the keep."

"Yes, Banphrionsa!" acknowledged Whitesky. "Glastoir," he beckoned to one of his captaens. The Banphrionsa wants to gain access inside of Dragonsbane Keep. The gate is located in the southern wall. Have your scouts search to the south of us and see if there is a way through the dolmaari encampment," Whitesky instructed them.

"Tá, Bánspéir Ceannasaí," he said with a salute of hitting his chest above his heart with his right fist. He rode back to his platoon.

About thirty minutes later, Glastoir returned. "Bánspéir Ceannasaí," said Glastoir, "there is no clear way through for a force of our size, but we did find an area of weakness. We should be able to break through their lines at that point with minimal casualties." Glastoir pointed off in a direction to the southwest.

Whitesky sighed. "I guess that will have to do."

Drake sat atop his steed facing the amassed force of the one hundred infantry of the Dwarven Envoy and nine hundred of the keep's soldiers. Del, atop his steed, was next to him. "Lord Darkstone!" Drake called.

A too-tall dwarf with a long, white beard ran from the assembled dwarves up to Drake and Del. "Yes, Lord Drake?"

"Lady Silvervale has arrived with a small force of aelf cavalry. We are going to create a diversion to allow the aelf to gain entrance to the keep."

"Aye, Lord Drake. My men are ready to teach these bawbags a lesson or two about how dangerous it is to execute a cowardly siege such as this."

"Very good, Lord Darkstone," replied Drake. "We will assemble outside the gate and form a Boar's Tooth formation. The tip of the Boar's Tooth will be where your dwarves and our soldiers will meet in the middle. You will take the eastern flank of the enemy. Del will lead our forces on the western flank. Go prepare your forces."

"Ja, Lord Drake!" answered Lord Darkstone. He ran back to his forces.

Drake marched out of the gate at the head of the dwarven column of heavy infantry. The dwarves carried their large shields in front of them to protect them from possible enemy projectiles.

Del led his infantry outside the keep behind the dwarven phalanx. According to his plan, he led his mass of soldiers to the southwest of the keep to engage the dolmaari on that side. The men marched nervously toward the large mass of the enemy. They knew what was in store for them when they reached the dolmaari. However, Del had them trained well enough that they would not break and run. The soldiers at the front were armed with large tower shields and long swords. The hope was that the tower shields would give them some degree of protection against the much taller dolmaari. The front rank could stab at the enemy between small gaps in the tower shields. Behind the first row of soldiers were two rows of soldiers armed with spears. They would use the spears to stab at the dolmaari above the shields of the first rank. That was the idea, at least. No army had ever fought this sort of war before. Behind the spearmen were several ranks of pikemen interspersed with halberdiers.

When the dwarven and human forces had assembled into their Boar's Tooth outside the front gate, Drake gave the command, "Charge!"

The dwarves exclaimed, "Zwerge für immer!" Then they immediately sprinted past Drake toward the dolmaari on the southeast side of the keep. They maintained their tight formation as they raced toward the enemy. The front rank kept their shields in front of them while the ranks behind them held their shields above their heads to prevent projectiles from raining down on them. Within minutes, the dwarves reached the front ranks of the dolmaari. The front rank of dwarves held fast with their large shields in front of them while the second rank began hacking away at the eight-foot tall dolmaari warriors with their two-handed battleaxes. The dolmaari were unprepared for the incredible force of the sprinting dwarves and immediately began to give ground.

At first it appeared the dwarves would quickly overwhelm the dolmaari, but the dolmaari were able to recover and began standing their ground again. Within the first minute of combat, thirty dolmaari soldiers lay dead on the field, while not a single dwarf had fallen. Once the dolmaari had recovered, however, they began to inflict casualties of their own. First one dwarf fell, then another. Each time a dwarf succumbed to his wounds, another dwarf would step up to fill in the line. This continued for some time. Cries of "Zwerge für immer!" continued to ring out in the early morning air. The dwarves were inflicting three casualties for every one they took, but that would not be enough in the long run.

At the same moment that the dwarves charged, the infantry surged past Del, all the while staying in formation. There was a massive clanging sound as the dolmaari reached out with their large hands and ripped their tower shields from them. Within an instant, half of the first rank was down, either dead or too injured to be of much use for the battle. The second rank of soldiers screamed in terror as they suddenly saw the large dolmaari standing right in front of them. They jabbed at them with their pikes, but their weapons were easily swatted away and the dolmaari brought down huge swaths of men with sweeping arcs of their four-clawed hands. The army of Dragonsbane were mere mosquitoes trying to bite a giant. The dolmaari began to move forward into the human army. It soon appeared as if they would be routed; however, at that instant, a volley of arrows rained down upon the advancing dolmaari. Del looked back at the keep and could see the grendlaar archers at the battlements. The volley of arrows appeared to give the dolmaari pause, but only for a moment. After their brief hesitation, they resumed their forward progress into the human ranks and continued their path of devastation.

Del yelled from the top of his horse, "Hold the line! Hold the line!" For now, his army was not being routed, but he didn't know how much longer it would stay that way.

∽∾

Laaran stood, observing, behind the battlement at the front gate. He had done one last sweep through the keep looking for any more dolmaari intruders. Having not found any, he was confident they had accounted for them all. Now he observed the combat at the south of the keep. The dwarves and Drake seemed to be holding their own for now. Del and the army of Dragonsbane Keep, however, was quite a different story. They were being mowed down like a farmer with a scythe cutting down the prairie grass. It looked like the dolmaari were inflicting ten deaths for each one that the Dragonsbane army was inflicting. The archers on the southern wall were evening the odds by a little, but it wouldn't be enough. Soon the entire force of Dragonsbane Keep would be decimated if something wasn't done.

"Korjinn, keep watch on the battle. I'll be back soon," Laaran said.

"Of course, Lord Laaran," replied Korjinn.

With that, Laaran nimbly jumped on the ladder and rode it down to the ground. He ran through the keep to the north until he reached the northern wall. He quickly spotted Zevirilyn on the catwalk above. "Zevirilyn!" he called. Zevirilyn looked down at Laaran. "I need you to send ten of your fire mages with me to the southern wall immediately. Our forces there are being overrun."

"Of course, Lord Laaran," Zevirilyn replied. Zevirilyn quickly assigned ten of his mages to accompany Laaran. They immediately began to descend the ladder. Once all were on the ground, they made their way toward the front gate with Laaran. He directed the ten mages up the staircase to man the battlements and followed them up.

⁓❧

Silvervale and Whitesky sat on their mounts looking for some sign that Drake had started the distraction to enable them to lead the aelf force into the keep.

"Look!" exclaimed Whitesky. "That small force of dolmaari is moving to the southwest. I think that's our sign." Whitesky turned to one of his captaens. "Lead the way, Glastoir." Glastoir and Ìoncaonach started toward the south. Whitesky drew his sabre and gave the silent signal to advance by raising it high above his head and swiping it forward. The column of cavalry advanced to the south.

In ten minutes, Whitesky and Silvervale had the aelf positioned roughly fifty yards away from the dolmaari. There appeared to be about five hundred of the dolmaari directly ahead of them. *This is the weak point in the lines*, Silvervale thought. *I would hate to see the strong point.* In the distance beyond the dolmaari directly in front of them, they could see fighting in the distance between dwarves and dolmaari.

Whitesky looked to the aelf behind him to determine their readiness. Then he turned to face the dolmaari and gave the command to charge with two quick swipes above his head with his sabre. At once, the entire branch of cavalry kicked their horses into a gallop and cried, "Bua nó bá!" Victory or death.

The cavalry column widened out to form a larger front. The riders at the front took hold of their spears and set them to ride down the dolmaari. The aelf in the rear rank took out their short bows and began shooting arrows in high arcs over the heads of their comrades in front of them, hitting the dolmaari with stunning force. One arrow alone did not appear enough to take them down, but it did stagger them a little. Some arrows, however, just seemed to glance off the dolmaari's armor-like skin.

The front line of cavalry rode into the dolmaari with a crushing force. Several dolmaari fell, spears protruding from their heads. The aelf who lost their spears drew their swords without delay. The dolmaari, of course, did not stand idly by and wait to be mowed down by the aelf. They swung their large clawed hands at the cavalrymen, unhorsing several of them. The aelf who made it through the dolmaari lines turned their horses around and charged at the dolmaari again, some of them striking with their spears for the first time, others with their newly drawn swords.

Silvervale saw a large concentration of dolmaari to the left of the aelf lines. They were far from any aelf at this time, but they were quickly closing the gap. Silvervale needed to do something powerful quickly. She muttered an incantation in aelf. Streaks of lightning crashed down from the sky onto these dolmaari. In an instant, fifty dolmaari lay dead on the turf, their bodies smoking.

However, another large force emerged from behind the ones Silvervale had killed. The spell she had just cast took a lot of energy out of her, and she would not be able to cast it again. "Brace your men, Whitesky! Here they come!"

"Athchruinníonn chun liom!" Whitesky shouted at his host. The aelf immediately began to rally around Whitesky, forming a line to face the oncoming dolmaari. "Cúiseamh!" At his signal, the entire force of aelf cavalry began to move as one, charging toward the enemy.

Drake observed the fighting from behind the dwarven lines. The dwarves were able to make progress against the dolmaari lines, but the human forces to his right were not faring well at all. Drake looked off to his left and noticed a large force of dolmaari break off from the line the dwarves were fighting and move to the east. When he peered into the distance, he noticed a line of cavalry charging toward the oncoming dolmaari. Drake seriously doubted the aelf had the numbers to survive a charge from that many dolmaari. He looked back to his right to locate Del. He saw him on his horse shouting orders to the human army. "Del!" he shouted. He swung his sword in circles around his head indicating he wanted to meet. Del nodded in acknowledgement. They both immediately kicked their warhorses into a gallop to confer.

"What is it, Drake?" asked Del when they met.

"Part of the dolmaari lines on my side have broken off to engage Silvervale's forces to the east. I want to shift the eastern flank of the dwarven infantry toward that direction to open a hole for Silvervale's cavalry to get inside the keep. I'm worried about the effect it will have on your troops."

"Don't worry about me or my men, Drake. I think I may have discovered a weakness which we can exploit."

"Do you care to elaborate?"

"Let's just say I've learned the armor on the backsides of the dolmaari is not as tough as the front side."

"Excellent! I'll leave you to it, then!" Del turned his horse and rode back toward his men. Drake rode back to behind the dwarven lines. "Lord Darkstone!" Drake called.

Moments later, Lord Darkstone emerged from the dwarven lines and ran up to Drake. "Ja, what is it, Lord Drake?"

"We need to shift the focus of our attack to the east in order to reach Silvervale and the aelf cavalry. I propose we form a Boar's Tooth of our own with the dwarven infantry and drive the point of that boar's tooth to the southeast."

"Aye, Lord Drake. I'll see that it's done." Lord Darkstone pivoted back to his forces and began shouting orders as he ran back. The effect was almost immediate. The left and right flanks held fast while the middle of the line punched its way forward, driving back the dolmaari. The dwarven formation then angled its attack to the southeast, which started to separate the dolmaari forces.

Del began shouting orders when he got back to his men. "Get all the halberds to the front!" The men immediately began handing halberds to soldiers in the second rank. "Second rank, stick the halberd through a gap in the front rank, extend it beyond the legs of the dolmaari, then pull back on the halberd so that the hook catches the dolmaari in the calf."

The soldiers in the second rank began performing the maneuver Del had ordered. It appeared to work, at least initially. The dolmaari in the front rank were immediately brought to their knees. Once they were on their knees, the front rank with the tower shields were able to do a quick thrust with their long sword into their eyes to dispatch them. However, it didn't take long for the dolmaari to adapt to the new strategy. The dolmaari backed away from the front line and began heaving corpses of their comrades on top of each other. Once the stack was about three feet high, they climbed on top of the pile, reached over the front rank, and slashed halberdsmen with their long talons. One by one, the halberdiers began to fall, allowing the dolmaari to advance once again on the human army. Within an instant, half of the first rank was down, either dead or too injured to be of much use for the battle. The second rank of soldiers screamed in terror as they suddenly saw the large dolmaari standing right in front of them. They jabbed at them with their spears, but their weapons were easily swatted away as the dolmaari slashed at them with all four arms, gutting some of the men like fish. Suddenly, explosions of fire erupted behind the dolmaari lines. This instantly through the dolmaari forces on the western flank into mass confusion. Del looked up at the battlements to see Laaran surrounded by fire mages. Del gave Laaran a nod. The confusion lasted only a moment, however. A high-pitched chittering erupted all around the soldiers, and the dolmaari returned to their ranks and continued their inexorable advance into the army of humans.

"For Dragonsbane and the Elemental Lord of Fire!" Del looked in the direction of the shouting. He couldn't believe what he saw. Dozens of soldiers on horses galloped up to the battlefront. The foot soldiers in the rear ranks were hastily trying to get out of the way of the charging horses. "Lord Del, we'll cover your retreat into the keep."

"Well met, Garaz! You've made a timely arrival."

"We can discuss it when we're all safely inside the keep. Fire warriors, on me!" Garaz shouted to his men. The fire warriors maneuvered their war horses through the foot soldiers and formed a line between the dolmaari and the keep.

Del turned toward his men and shouted, "Withdraw into the keep!" His men immediately began to rapidly back up toward the keep.

The fire warriors and war horses were trained for exactly this sort of combat, and they were able to successfully hold off the dolmaari until the foot soldiers were a safe distance away. "Fire warriors. Fire burst on the front rank. Fire bursts all along the line immediately exploded, engulfing both the dolmaari and the fire warriors. This sudden change of tactic threw the dolmaari into disarray. High-pitched cries erupted from the dolmaari as they broke away from their formations once again. Garaz and his fire warriors used the distraction to slowly retreat into the keep.

The charging aelf cavalry slammed into the first rank of dolmaari. Some of the dolmaari fell, but most held their ground as the cavalry galloped past. Another large group of dolmaari was bearing down on the aelf. They immediately spun their horses around and raced back the way they had come, attacking the dolmaari from behind as they passed them. This attack was much more successful. Several of the dolmaari collapsed to the ground on the return attack. Once clear of the dolmaari, Whitesky cried out, "Athchruinníonn chun liom!" Whitesky's cavalry reformed quickly, albeit it with fewer aelf than at the start of the attack.

"Look!" exclaimed Silvervale. "Drake is leading the dwarves in this direction. This is the opening we've been waiting for."

Silvervale and Whitesky watched in amazement as the dwarven infantry smashed into the rear of the large force of dolmaari that had been coming after the aelf. The dwarves swung their heavy battleaxes in large arcs, each cutting down a dolmaari every few seconds. The dolmaari facing the aelf, realizing the greater threat, turned to confront the dwarves. Seeing this as a sign, Whitesky ordered, "Cúiseamh!" The aelf cavalry immediately charged the backs of the dolmaari. With the dwarven heavy infantry on one side and the aelf cavalry on the other, the dolmaari didn't stand a chance. Within several minutes, nearly five hundred dolmaari lay dead. Only a handful of aelf and no dwarves suffered the same fate.

Drake rode up to Silvervale. "Well met, Princess!"

"Very well met, indeed, Drake," she responded.

The dolmaari began regrouping from the vice maneuver inflicted on them by the dwarves and aelf. They lined up shoulder-to-shoulder and began marching once again toward the combined forces of the aelf and dwarves.

"We should make haste into the keep while the dolmaari are in retreat," Drake suggested. I'll cover our retreat. Drake turned back toward the oncoming dolmaari. He held his gauntleted hands out in front of him and began to slowly rotate them back and forth. He focused intently on the ground in front of him. Without warning, a wall of fire ten feet tall, five feet wide, and one hundred feet long appeared in front of Drake. The dolmaari instantly stopped their advance.

Drake turned back to Whitesky, who nodded to Drake. Whitesky then commanded his men to ride hard to the keep. The dwarves followed behind the cavalry. In a short time, all the forces of Dragonsbane were inside the keep with the gate barred. Del approached Drake with Garaz in tow. Garaz and Del immediately dismounted and Silvervale and Whitesky followed suit.

"Drake, Del, this is Whitesky, the commander of the aelf cavalry." Del nodded a greeting.

"Well met, Lord Whitesky!" Drake then turned to Del. "We need to have a council meeting immediately. Let's meet in the council room in thirty minutes. Lord Whitesky and Garaz, would you please join us?" Garaz nodded his assent.

"Of course, Lord Drake!" answered Whitesky. "But I am not a lord."

"After this, you will be," Drake stated matter-of-factly. "Lord Darkstone!"

"Ja, Lord Drake," said Darkstone as he approached the group.

"We are having a council meeting at the temple in thirty minutes. Would you please join us?"

"It would be my honor and duty, Lord Drake."

"I will see you all in thirty minutes," said Drake. The assembled leaders dispersed to get ready for the council meeting.

৯৹৶

The council of Dragonsbane Keep and Zevirilyn met in the conference room in the temple. This time they were joined by Lord Darkstone and Whitesky. Drake stood. "First off, I want to thank Garaz for his timely arrival with the contingent of fire warriors. It's likely our entire human infantry force would have been completely decimated had they not intervened. How is it that you came from the west when the Elemental Palace of Fire is to the east?"

"We saw a large force of aelf cavalry approaching from the east. We had to take a detour to the north to avoid the aelf and get around the dolmaari. I see now that the aelf were coming to our aid. I did not expect that. We could have arrived sooner if we had known they were friendly forces."

"I know we were hoping for more than one branch of Éodram cavalry to come to our aid, but we can't change the facts," Drake said. "We need to figure out what we are going to do next so that we all live through this. Elian, what are our food stores like?"

"We had about two weeks of food left to feed the garrison before the attack. However, because of the casualties we sustained, and taking into account the additional aelf and fire warriors within the walls, I would say we have approximately three weeks left. If we go on three quarters rations, we could extend for another week or so."

"So, we'll need to take action before that time. Laaran, have you determined how many dolmaari were killed in the attack?" asked Drake.

"It's a little difficult to say because their casualties were spread out all along the southern wall. However, a fairly good estimation would be around one thousand. Unless they've shifted their forces, that would leave approximately three thousand dolmaari on our southern flank. The dolmaari have all withdrawn to the tree line, so we're no longer able to see them."

"Understood. Lord Darkstone, how many of the dwarves were lost in the attack?"

"Ten great warriors have begun the Wild Hunt, Lord Drake."

"We thank your men for their sacrifice."

"Pfahh!" interjected Lord Darkstone. "They died the warrior's death, each taking three of those bawbags with them! It is a moment of joy and celebration, not sorrow!"

"Thank you, Lord Darkstone. Whitesky, how did your cavalry fare during the battle?"

"Lord Drake, after healing I should have about one hundred soldiers ready for battle again."

"Del, how many men do we have left after the battle?"

"After the foray, five hundred of our own men lay dead on the field," Del answered.

Everyone gasped at the news. "But that's over half of the force that was sent out."

"Yes, Elian, that is correct, but we cannot let that deter us. We must attack again!" exclaimed Del emphatically.

"I believe such an attack would be in vain," Drake countered. "Judging by the numbers lost on each side in an open field attack, we would lose a war of attrition."

"But it's better than starving to death inside these blasted walls!" thundered Del. "At least give us a chance!"

Drake held up his hand to quiet Del. "I think we have better options, however."

"Well, let's hear them, Drake," Del said.

"I think we need to goad the dolmaari into attacking us so that we will have the advantage of being behind the walls of the keep.

"However, we're vulnerable on the east and west walls because we never completed the catwalks on those sides. Therefore, I've talked to James, our chief engineer. He said we have enough lumber and supplies to complete a catwalk along the east and west walls. He estimates it will take approximately two weeks to complete both catwalks. I've directed him to begin work immediately."

Drake continued, "I propose we place fifty grendlaar archers each and fifty of the aelf armed with bows on the east and west walls. We will also place one hundred and fifty of our soldiers and trainees on each wall armed with pikes to repel any dolmaari that reach the top of walls. Additionally, we will station twenty-five fire warriors on each wall."

"What of the priests and fire mages, Drake?" inquired Silvervale.

"They're the key to all of this. We will position our Forest Spirit priests on the southern wall and our fire mages on the northern wall. They will unleash their spells in the trees and, hopefully, strike at the dolmaari. Either the dolmaari will retreat or they will begin an assault on the keep. Either way, we should be able to break this siege."

"But we can't see into the trees to target the dolmaari," Zevirilyn protested.

Elian spoke up in response. "It shouldn't matter. We can see the lights from their fires. If we just target the fires, we should hit at least some of the dolmaari. After that, they'll have to make a decision on what to do next."

Del nodded his head up and down. "This is a sound plan, Drake. But what of the dwarven infantry?"

"We'll hold them in reserve inside the walls. If the dolmaari overrun one of the walls, the dwarves can respond to that side. If the dolmaari manage to get inside the walls, they can confront that threat."

"So when do we begin the attack?" asked Laaran.

"We'll give James the two weeks he needs to complete the catwalks. Laaran, continue to scout around the outside to see if we see any movement from the dolmaari." Drake turned to Elian. "Elian, have your priests continue to prepare healing and offensive spells."

"I'll see to it," Elian responded.

"Zevirilyn, have your fire mages continue to prepare offensive spells as well."

"As you command, Lord Drake."

"Finally, Del and I will continue to train our new recruits. We will meet here in the morning in two weeks' time. You are all dismissed."

☨

Several single bolts of lightning streaked down from the early morning sky and struck the ground inside the tree line south of the keep. Elian watched from the gatehouse. Drake decided the attack would start in the early morning at the start of the fourth week from the day the aelf cavalry arrived. The Forest Spirit priests were well prepared for this attack. They had spent hours writing scrolls to use in the attack. Multiple bolt lightning strikes may have been more effective, but they took longer to create and took a lot more energy. Besides, since they couldn't see any of the dolmaari, they could well waste a powerful spell on empty ground.

After the initial barrage of lightning, the priests waited several minutes to see if there was any reaction from the dolmaari. Elian could not perceive any movement from the dolmaari lines. He supposed they were withdrawing or simply gone already. That last thought didn't seem likely. The dolmaari had exhibited great patience in conducting this siege for the past month or so. "Again!" ordered Elian.

Several more lightning bolts shot from the sky and struck the ground again. There still seemed to be no more movement from the dolmaari. Elian was beginning to wonder if this strategy of Drake's was going to work. Suddenly, a great eagle flew high above the wall. Elian followed it with his eyes. *What a magnificent creature!* thought Elian. *Too bad we can't have the creatures of the forest rise to our defense.* The eagle continued flying toward the northern wall.

Silvervale observed the eagle soaring overhead as she was watching for Elian's lightning attack from the south. Zevirilyn stood next to her. Upon seeing a set of lightning bolts streak down, she turned to Zevirilyn and said quietly, "Now, Zevirilyn."

"Strike!" Zevirilyn cried. The fire mages unleashed in an instant. Several bursts of fire erupted beyond the tree line on the north side of Dragonsbane Keep. "Hold!" commanded Zevirilyn. They waited for several minutes, but no dolmaari burst from the trees.

Silvervale was confused. This plan should have worked. *Could the dolmaari have broken off the siege?* she wondered to herself. *That wouldn't make any sense.* "Again," Silvervale said to Zevirilyn.

"Strike!" cried Zevirilyn once more. More fire bursts exploded in the trees north of the keep, but still no indication the dolmaari were even there.

"Laaran!" called Silvervale.

Laaran, who was just twenty feet from Silvervale on the catwalk, trotted over to her. "Yes? What is it, Silvervale?" he asked.

"Go inform Drake that there does not appear to be any evidence that the dolmaari are where we thought they were. I have seen no reaction from them."

"At once!" Laaran declared as he spun on his toes and dashed down the catwalk toward the west. He turned at the corner onto the newly constructed catwalk. "Drake!" he called as he ran up to him.

"Yes, what is it, Laaran?"

"Silvervale says she sees no evidence the firebursts are doing anything. There has been no reaction from the dolmaari."

"Go to the front gate and tell Elian to come here."

"On my way! He'll come faster than a virgin with the king's prized concubine," Laaran called as he sprinted down the catwalk toward the front gate.

Laaran arrived with Elian in a matter of minutes. "Elian, have you seen any reaction from the dolmaari after the lightning attack?" Drake asked.

"No."

"Then, satisfy my curiosity and cast one of those multiple lightning bolt spells just beyond the tree line to the west."

"But I thought you said—"

"Indulge me," Drake interrupted Elian.

"Very well." Elian turned to look over the wall and muttered an incantation. Within seconds, several bolts of lightning burst from the sky, striking the ground below. Instantly, high-pitched cries rang out in the early morning fog.

"I think we've found where they went," Drake stated.

"They must have changed positions during the night," Laaran reasoned.

"Now we wait to see what happens next," said Drake.

For a long while, Drake, Laaran, and Elian looked off to the western tree line but could see no movement from the dolmaari. "Curious," said Drake.

Laaran leaned over the parapet and peered into the low light. "I think I see something."

"What is it? What do you see?" asked Drake.

Elian peered in the same direction and said, "Oh, I think I see it, too."

"I still can't see anything," declared Drake. "What is it?"

"It's like the ground is undulating," answered Laaran. "The ground looks the same, but it appears to be moving slightly up and down."

"Camouflage?" asked Elian. "Hold on a moment." Elian put the fingertips of both hands on his temples and incanted, "Soiléir amharc!" His eyes immediately began to glow a bright yellow. "I can see them now. They are moving at an incredibly fast speed. They've already covered half the ground between here and the tree line."

Del turned to Laaran. "Laaran, return to Silvervale and instruct her to go to the east wall. Tell her to cast the same spell Elian just cast and see if we are being attacked from that side as well."

"You got it, boss!" Laaran sprinted back along the catwalk to the north side of the keep. He immediately ran up to Silvervale.

"What is it, Laaran?" Silvervale asked.

"Del asked you to come with me to the east side of the keep. I have something to show you." Without even waiting for a response from Silvervale, Laaran raced toward the east side of the keep. Silvervale followed along as fast as she could.

After rounding the northeast corner of the keep, Laaran immediately darted toward Drake. "We have a problem, Drake."

"What is it?"

"Wait for Silvervale to get here. She can describe it better than I can." Laaran looked over the wall to the east of the keep and could see the same undulating vision he had on the west side.

Silvervale arrived breathless. "What is going on, Laaran?"

"Look over the wall and cast the spell that allows you to see things that most people can't see."

Silvervale incanted, "Soiléir amharc!" and touched her temples. Her eyes immediately began to glow just as Elian's had. She looked over the wall as Laaran had instructed. "In ainm Faraois Biotáillí!" she uncharacteristically swore.

"What is it?" Drake asked urgently.

"The entire dolmaari army is advancing across the open ground between the tree line and the wall." Silvervale looked straight down the wall. "They have already reached the wall!"

"How is this possible?" Drake asked.

"They have some way to camouflage their backs," Laaran explained.

"Laaran, we need some of the mages on this wall immediately!"

"Alright, Drake, but you and Del will owe me a new pair of boots after this!" Laaran said as he ran back along the catwalk to the north wall.

"Silvervale, is there a spell you can cast to kill those dolmaari that are already at our wall?" Drake asked.

"The only spell that would work is lightning, but I fear it will also damage the wall."

"Very well. Archers, I know you can't see the dolmaari right now, but just aim straight down, and we'll try to kill them before they find a way to scale the wall."

The archers began to loose arrows toward the base of the wall. High-pitched screaming immediately followed, indicating at least some of the arrows were hitting their mark. However, loud thunking noises could soon be heard coming up from the ground. Drake looked over the wall. He was able to see them now because he wasn't looking at their backs, and he exclaimed, "They're scaling the wall!"

"How are they doing that?" asked Silvervale

"They're using their talons to grip into the wall."

Silvervale looked over the wall. "They are moving phenomenally fast!"

Laaran returned with several fire mages in tow.

"Quickly, throw some fire bursts along the wall!" Drake ordered.

The fire mages instantly complied. This caused the initial wave of dolmaari to crash to the ground. However, the dolmaari kept coming. Silvervale cast a burst lightning spell over the open ground. She could see this killed scores of them, but they still kept coming. The fire mages continued to cast fire bursts, which successfully sent more dolmaari hurtling to the ground. But it wasn't enough. The dolmaari made steady progress toward the top of the wall. This sent the grendlaar archers into a panic, and they began to flee the catwalk to the ground below, inside the keep.

"Cowards!" Drake cried as they fled. "Men and aelf, prepare to defend the wall with pikes and swords!"

The human soldiers of Dragonsbane Keep dropped their bows and picked up the pikes as the aelf dropped their bows and drew their swords. The first wave of dolmaari reached the top of the wall. The pikemen and aelf tried to repel them from getting over the wall, but it was to no avail. The dolmaari were firmly attached to the wall with their talons. The pikes and swords also proved mostly ineffective against the natural armor of the dolmaari. The dolmaari used the talons of their upper two arms to slash indiscriminately at the defenders, killing some of them instantly, or knocking them off the catwalk to fall to their deaths on the ground below. Fire and lightning bursts continued to destroy dolmaari in the open ground on the east of the keep, but it didn't seem to even make a dent in the constant horde of dolmaari.

"Men, rally around me!" Drake shouted. "We need to make a defensive withdrawal, or we'll be overrun!" The men and aelf around Drake took defensive stances as they backed away to the northeast corner. "Whitesky! Rally the men on your side and make a defensive withdrawal to the southeast corner."

Whitesky nodded his understanding and cried, "Men, on me!" The men and aelf around Whitesky immediately rallied around him as they began their defensive withdrawal.

Dolmaari continued to pour over the walls. "Fire warriors!" screamed Drake. "Throw up walls of fire along the top of the wall to prevent any more dolmaari from getting on the catwalk." Several walls of fire erupted along the top of most of the eastern wall, each beginning where the previous stopped. However, that did nothing for the dolmaari already on the catwalk. There was no space to move. The entire platform was filled with men, aelf, and dolmaari. The catwalk began to sway. Then a loud crack was heard as the platform began to fall away into the keep. "Brace yourselves!" Drake called out.

Silvervale, seeing the imminent danger, whispered a quick spell and floated like a feather to the ground, unharmed. The same could not be said of the others. The catwalk made a deafening thud as it crashed to the ground. Of the dozens of men and aelf who were on the catwalk when it fell, only a handful were still moving on the ground. Many dolmaari also lay unmoving on the ground. *Where is Drake?* Silvervale thought. Then she saw him. He was lying motionless on the ground. She saw Laaran walking, apparently unhurt. *How did Laaran manage to land on the ground completely unharmed?* she wondered. "Laaran!"

she called out. Laaran looked in her direction. "Quickly, run to Del and tell him what has happened."

Laaran gave no reply, but immediately sprinted toward the western wall. "Whitesky!" He heard Silvervale scream. He heard no reply.

As Laaran ran, he passed by Lord Darkstone. "Be prepared for the dolmaari to come flooding over the eastern wall."

"Aye, Lord Laaran. We'll be ready for the Scheissfressers."

Laaran reached the base of the catwalk on the western wall. "Del!" he called up.

Del immediately stuck his head out over the railing.

"We've lost the eastern wall. The catwalk completely collapsed. Dozens are dead or incapacitated," he called up to Del.

"So that was the enormous crash we heard. What about Drake?"

Laaran shook his head. "Out of the fight. Dead or unconscious, I'm not sure which."

"Damn it all!" exclaimed Del.

"How goes it up there?" Laaran asked.

"We've slowed them a bit, but they'll reach the wall soon."

"I suggest you withdraw your forces to the ground now."

"No! We can fend them off!"

"Del, they *will* reach the top of the wall. And when they do, the added weight of the dolmaari on the catwalk will cause it to collapse, the same as it did to ours. Preserve the lives so that they can fight on the ground."

"I suppose what you say has wisdom," agreed Del. "Very well." Del turned to the men and aelf on the catwalk. "Men, we will strategically withdraw to the grounds inside the keep." Del looked down to Laaran again. "Laaran, inform those still on the catwalks on the north and south sides of the keep to withdraw to the ground." Laaran nodded and ran off to the south side of the keep.

Del, with Elian at his side, led the withdrawal of the men and aelf. They all managed to get to the ground safely. Del and Elian immediately sought out Lord Darkstone, who approached Del. "So what's the plan then, Lord Del?"

"First, we need to move our injured from the ground to the temple. Have your forces cover our eastern flank while Elian and the Forest Spirit priests gather the wounded."

Lord Darkstone saluted. "Ja, I'll see it done! Alright, men. Follow me. Let's keep these poor excuses for donkey foreskins from getting any farther into the keep." The dwarves immediately formed a defensive flank on the east.

Silvervale frantically ran to Del. "Del, Drake is down. Alive, but unconscious. I do not know where Whitesky is."

"We'll take care of the wounded as soon as the priests get here." Laaran ran up to Del with the Forest Spirit priests behind him. Del turned to Elian. "Take command of the priests and get our wounded in the temple for healing."

"Of course," responded Elian. He turned to the priests. "Let's search through the bodies to find anyone still alive." Elian and the priests moved off to sort through the wounded.

"Laaran, get the mages from the northern wall and bring them here," Del directed. Laaran dashed off to the north. Del looked to Silvervale. "Silvervale, when the mages get here, you and Zevirilyn take command of them and defend our western flank. Throw whatever you've got at them. Don't worry about damaging the wall. The wall won't do us any good if we're all dead."

"Understood," acknowledged Silvervale.

The dolmaari on the eastern flank reached the line of dwarves. The dolmaari lashed out at the dwarves with all four limbs in a flurry. However, the dwarves stood firm and did not give the dolmaari even an inch. Behind the dwarven line, Elian and the priests hurriedly made their way through the casualties. They found relatively few survivors among those who were on the catwalk when it collapsed.

"Here they come!" screamed Laaran. Del looked back to the west to see the first dolmaari coming over the western wall. The mages arriving from the northern wall began to unleash their fire and lighting spells on the invading horde, leaving scores of dolmaari dead. However, the dolmaari did not stop coming over the wall. For every one felled by fire or lightning, three more came over the wall in replacement.

Del looked back to the east. The dolmaari were slowly beginning to push the dwarves back. Fortunately, it looked as if Elian and the priests were nearly done collecting the injured. Del spun around to look in all directions. The swarm of dolmaari seemed to pulse as they slowly began to surround the last defenders of Dragonsbane Keep. The dolmaari had reached the lines of mages, who were falling like scrub trees to a battle axe. "Gods," Del muttered. "So this is how it all ends." He took a moment to calm himself and gather his resolve. "Let's send these sons of goat whores back to whatever hell they came from!" He screamed to the men and aelf around him. Del thrust both his arms above his hand, a long sword gripped in each hand. "Charge!" he screamed and ran toward the oncoming dolmaari. The aelf and men around Del cheered and joined in the charge toward the host of dolmaari.

The initial impact of the charging men and aelf actually knocked the line of dolmaari back a few paces. The dolmaari quickly recovered, however, and once again began their slow advance on the forces of Dragonsbane Keep. The last guardians of the keep were surrounded by the dolmaari in a circle about one hundred feet in diameter.

Suddenly, horns in the east erupted in the air. Time seemed to stop for just a moment. The horn was echoed by another one in the west. Then, unbelievably, the dolmaari began to withdraw. Del couldn't understand it. The dolmaari were on the brink of wiping out the entire garrison of Dragonsbane Keep. Why would they start to withdraw? And what were those horns?

"Those are aelf trumpets!" exclaimed Silvervale. "We are saved!"

Del turned to his right. "Laaran, get to the catwalk on the north wall and see what's happening outside."

Laaran immediately darted off in that direction. When he got there, he swung a rope up to the catwalk. The grappling hook caught on a railing post. Laaran nimbly climbed the rope to the top. He stood on the catwalk, surveying the land outside the keep. He saw an incredible force of cavalry attacking the dolmaari from behind. On both east and west flanks, the dolmaari were falling to the heavy cavalry like wheat to a scythe. The dolmaari were trapped between the cavalry and the walls of Dragonsbane Keep. Laaran looked back inside the keep. Nearly all the dolmaari had fled back over the walls. The dwarves were still pursuing the injured dolmaari survivors and cutting them down. Laaran jumped off the catwalk, grabbed hold of his rope, and slid back down to the ground. He ran back to Del to report his observations.

Del, looking completely exhausted, called, "Lord Darkstone! To me!"

Lord Darkstone broke off from his attacking force and hustled up to Del. "Yes, Lord Del?"

"It appears we are saved. Aelf heavy cavalry have arrived and have begun a rout of the dolmaari. How many infantry do you have remaining?"

"There be about seventy-five still able to fight!"

"Please have your dwarves join me at the front gate. We will assist the aelf in the ground assault of the dolmaari."

"It would be me pleasure, Lord Del! We can ensure these bawbags have their final reckoning with Nidhogg in Niflheim." Lord Darkstone ran off toward the dwarves while shouting orders to gather his infantry.

With the dwarven infantry on one side and an entire trunk of High Aelf forces on the other, the battle was soon over. After two hours of heavy combat, all remaining dolmaari still alive were sent fleeing into the forest in all directions.

The following morning, the leaders of the defending forces of Dragonsbane Keep met in the council chamber in the temple. "It appears the defense of Dragonsbane Keep has been successful," Drake began weakly, still recovering from his injuries. "If it were not for the timely intervention of the aelf cavalry, we certainly would have been overcome."

"Do not think this means we are allies, human," spoke up a silver-haired aelf. "Our only mission was to return the Banphrionsa to the High King safely. Those creatures simply stood between us and the princess."

"We thank you all the same, Prince Silverhaven," Drake responded.

"We would like to depart now with the Banphrionsa," Silverhaven declared.

"What? Brother, I did not agree to this," argued Silvervale.

"Nevertheless, our father wishes it, and I will ensure it happens," Silverhaven retorted.

Del jumped up from his chair. "If Silvervale does not wish to return, then she will stay here," he firmly declared. The corner of Silverhaven's mouth curled into a smirk.

"Del, please sit down," urged Drake. "We do not wish to cause further animosity between us and the aelf."

"But I still do not want to go," Silvervale protested.

Whitesky, sitting next to Silvervale, spoke up, "Please, Íoncroí, consider returning with me. We can use this as an opportunity to rekindle our friendship."

Silvervale sat quietly and thought about this. With her green eyes, she peered into Whitesky's eyes. Everyone in the room was awaiting her answer. After several moments, she said, "Very well. I will return at this time." She then looked up at Silverhaven. "But know, brother, this will not be forever. I *will* return here someday." Silverhaven merely grunted in response.

"Lord Darkstone," began Drake, "what is your plan?"

"We will return immediately to the White Hills and tell stories of great glory with the heroes of Dragonsbane Keep."

"May the Elemental Lord of Earth see you safely home," said Drake. "Now for those of us remaining, let us see to the repair and recovery of Dragonsbane Keep. I thank you all and wish the Forest Spirits and the Elemental Lords give blessings to you all."

৯৽৵

*And so the tale would be told for generations to come: the story of how humans, aelf, dwarves, grendlaar, elementalists, and adherents of the Forest Spirits united for one common cause. However, the aelf told the tale a different way: the High Aelf had come to destroy the human enclave, but had spared them out of their beneficent mercy. Whichever tale you believe, it appeared the founders of Dragonsbane Keep were one step closer to creating a freehold where those of all races and belief systems could live together in harmony. What would the future hold? Only time would tell.*

The End

# LOLARK THE VALIANT
by
Roger Stockman

"Up and at 'em!" a booming voice rang out through the barracks. Muted half groans greeted Sir Lolark the Valiant as the paladins groggily woke up from their deep slumber. "Get your gear packed up for a campaign lasting at least several days. Muster up in the parade ground in one hour." Lolark spun around on his heels as the paladins in the barracks slowly roused themselves. On his way out, he noticed a young paladin standing at the foot of his bed already fully clothed and saluting Lolark as he walked by. Lolark stopped at the young man and turned to face him. Due to his great height, Lolark had to squat down in order to look eye-to-eye with the young paladin.

"What is your name, young sir?"

"Benjamin, sir," he said, his voice cracking.

Lolark rested a hand on Benjamin's left shoulder. "It's *Sir* Benjamin. Now do you want to try that again, son? What is your name?"

"Sir Benjamin," he said with a slightly more confident tone.

"That's much better, son. I admire your pro-activeness. It will serve you well in the future."

"Thank you, sir!" Benjamin said with an air of pride in his voice.

"Carry on, soldier."

"Yes, sir!" Benjamin said with a salute. Lolark returned the salute and turned to leave.

He ducked to exit through the doorway as he was too tall to fit under the jamb. This was the fifth and final barracks he visited this early morning. Each barracks held a spear of two hundred paladins each. Most of the paladins in this phalanx were fairly new to the Order of the Silver Cross paladins. In fact, over eighty percent of the paladins in this phalanx had been members of the order for just over a year.

Once he exited the barracks, Lolark steered himself toward the meeting hall of Silver Cross Keep. He had a meeting with his spear commanders to brief them on their upcoming mission. As soon as Lolark entered the room, all five of them immediately jumped to their feet and stood at attention.

"As you were," Lolark commanded. The commanders immediately took their seats. Lolark walked to the other side of the round table where his chair waited. Because he was too large for the ordinary chairs, they built him a special chair, and he sat in it.

Without so much as a pause, Lolark began, "Very well, let's get to it, shall we? Our mission is to go to the aid of the town of Westmoor." Lolark stood as he placed his hand on Westmoor on the map spread out on the table. "Our scouts have reported a large force of grendlaar and their grackle commanders emerging from the hills to the north. There are possibly five thousand in this force. Their apparent destination is Westmoor. I know that all of you have been on several of these missions before, so I won't bore you with the details. Our goal is to make it to Westmoor before the grendlaar forces and defend the town. This is a fairly routine mission, so I don't expect we'll be gone for more than a week, barring any unforeseen circumstances. Are there any questions?"

"Yes, sir," spoke up Sir Philip, commander of the second spear. Why aren't the knights of Blue Keep responding to this threat? Their journey there would be significantly shorter than ours.

"That is a good question, Sir Philip. Apparently, there is another large group of grendlaar approaching Cairthorn. The knights of Blue Keep have been called to respond to that threat," said Lolark.

"And what of the paladins of Gold Keep?" asked Sir Damon, commander of the third spear. "Their keep lies between grendlaar lands and Cairthorn. Couldn't they intercept this second grendlaar force before they reach Cairthorn?"

"The Gold Keep Paladins are on a separate mission in the Venting Mountains," answered Lolark. The commanders all nodded with understanding. "Are there any further questions?"

Lolark encountered silence and the stoic faces of his commanders. "Very well. Have your spears mustered in the parade ground ready to depart in one hour. You are dismissed." The commanders stood up in unison, saluted Lolark, and, one-by-one, departed the meeting room.

✤

Lolark sat atop his warhorse, Lion, a light-brown Friesian. He watched the paladins as they mustered into their respective spears. They stood shoulder-to-shoulder in ten ranks of twenty paladins, which made up one spear. There were five such formations in front of Lolark; each of the formations had its spear commander in front, sitting on a warhorse overseeing the muster.

Each of the paladins, Lolark included, was clad in full plate armor with a long sword belted at his or her waist. Lolark commanded this phalanx of one thousand paladins on this mission. He had been training them to work together as a cohesive fighting unit for the past year. He was confident that they were ready for this mission.

The war with the grendlaar had been raging, off and on, for the past one hundred and fifty years, and it showed no sign of stopping. It seemed the paladins and knights of Drascara were simply putting out fires one by one without bringing about any resolution. That's what they were doing today, putting out the most recent fire around Westmoor. Lolark was getting frustrated with his duty. He had been a paladin in the Order of the Silver Cross for ten years and mostly all he had done was fight grendlaar. He had risen to the rank of phalanx commander. Ten was a remarkably short time for one to reach the rank of phalanx commander, but Lolark had accomplished it through dedication. The Master and Commander of Silver Cross Keep had offered Lolark the quartermaster position, which technically wasn't a promotion. However, serving in that position would make it more likely for him to get promoted to Marshall sooner rather than later. He was seriously considering accepting the position after ten grueling years of fighting grendlaar.

"Spear commanders, report!" bellowed Lolark.

One by one, each of the spear commanders yelled back, "All present, sir!"

"Have your men mount up and meet in formation outside the keep!" Lolark ordered. Each spear commander turned to their spear and gave the order. The paladins immediately jumped into motion towards their respective stables. Leading: Spear commanders, on horseback, directed their men. Lolark rode Lion out the gate to await the phalanx.

ॐ

Within thirty minutes, the entire phalanx mustered itself on horseback outside Silver Cross Keep. Since Silver Cross Keep was a fairly affluent order, the horses were also well-armored and well-armed. Each horse had a full set of plate barding. Additionally, each horse was equipped with a lance, a mace, an axe, and a light crossbow with twenty bolts each. Each paladin also had a large shield strapped to his back. Lolark turned Lion toward the phalanx and shouted, "Move out!"

The first spear immediately began riding out while remaining in formation and took the lead of the phalanx. The remaining spears each fell in behind the formation until they were in a column approximately a quarter hursmarc long. Sir Lolark rode up beside his first spear commander, Sir Oliver the Honest. Sir Oliver had served under Lolark for the last five years, so they knew each other well. "It looks like we should have good enough weather to get to Westmoor," Lolark said.

"I'm a little suspicious of those clouds to the east," Oliver said as he pointed at the sky in that direction.

"Not to worry, old friend. Those clouds are a long way off. We should have plenty of time to reach Westmoor. Besides, the wind is blowing the other way"

"If you say so, Lolark," replied Oliver. "But the wind could switch directions at any time, and then we could be in for a real squall."

Lolark nodded. He had great trust in his first spear commander. He knew that even if Sir Oliver was right about the weather, he could depend on Oliver to adapt to the situation. They rode in silence for a while after that.

After two hours of riding, Oliver turned to Lolark. "Can you feel that, Lolark?"

"Yes," Lolark replied thoughtfully. "The wind is shifting. We should pick up the pace to outrun the storm. Send your scout to the second spear to inform them."

"Yes, Lolark!" Oliver turned to his left. "Lady Sophia!" he called. A paladin on horseback rode up to Oliver.

"Yes, sir?"

"Ride to the second spear and tell them we're going to pick up the pace to get beyond the storm. Have the message passed all the way to the rear"

"Yes, sir!" Sophia said with a salute and immediately rode toward the north."

They immediately traveled at a slow trot. Within thirty minutes, the wind picked up. The banner with the silver cross on a royal blue background whipped around violently. Then the rain started. Thunder rumbled in the distance, and Lolark saw fork lightning erupting from the clouds in the west. "Sir Oliver, send a banner of soldiers into those foothills to look for the safest place to set up a camp and wait out this storm." Lolark pointed to the south at the emerging foothills.

"Yes, Sir Lolark!" Oliver turned to his spear. "First banner!" he called out. He gave them Lolark's order. Twenty armored paladins shot out of the formation like a bolt from a ballista and galloped to the south. The rest of the phalanx continued to ride in a slow trot. Fifteen minutes later, a lone rider galloped from the south. He rode directly up to Sir Oliver.

"Sir Jason, report!"

"Sir Oliver, we believe we have located a suitable location for an encampment. It's a low area between some hills that can buffet us from the winds. The other men have begun setting up an encampment."

"Very good, Sir Jason. Ride back to the second spear and tell them we're going to double time to that location."

"Yes, sir," Sir Jason said with a salute as he rode off.

Lolark turned his head back toward the phalanx and shouted with his booming voice, "Phalanx! Double time, march!" The entire first spear burst forth in unison. The horses' hooves created a cacophony that drowned out the thunder coming from the west.

It took over an hour for the entire phalanx to reach the position of the encampment. The paladins spent another thirty minutes creating a makeshift wall by embedding their large shields in the ground and staking them down. A shield wall now encompassed the entire encampment of one thousand paladins.

The paladins barely had time to hunker down behind their shields when the storm began in earnest. Large drops of rain pelted off the plate armor, creating a melody of tiny bells. The wind was getting much stronger now. Lolark, at the center of the encampment, watched as several large shields flew overhead from the west. "Brace yourselves!" Lolark commanded.

"Sir Lolark!" a paladin yelled. Lolark looked off in the direction of the voice. "Look!" the paladin screamed as he pointed off to the northeast.

Lolark looked in horror as a funnel cloud touched down from the sky and began heading in the direction of the north end of the encampment. "Stake yourselves to the ground if you can!" Lolark shouted to any who could hear his voice.

Lolark looked back in the direction of the funnel cloud and stared in disbelief as the tornado tore through the north end of the encampment. As the tornado picked up men and horses, terrified screams burst from the north as they were carried off to the east. Lolark guessed it was scores of men and horses. He muttered a silent prayer to himself, then he took his lance and some rope from Lion. After thrusting his lance into the ground, he tied himself to it as best he could.

Fifteen horrifying minutes passed before the storm finally passed them. Lolark stood and called out, "Spear commanders, report!" Sir Oliver and Sir Philip reported no casualties in their spears but quite an amount of lost gear and weapons.

"Sir Oliver, have a scout ride to the north to check on spears three, four, and five."

"Yes, Sir!" Sir Oliver turned around and gave the order to Lady Sophia, who rode off to the north. Within minutes, she returned with another rider on her horse.

The rider dismounted and stood at attention in front of Lolark. "Sir – "

"Roderick, sir." The paladin looked as if he had been the object of a laundress in a laundry tub. His armor showed dents in several places, and he had several cuts on his face.

"Sir Roderick, report. What is the status of spears three, four, and five?"

At first all Sir Roderick could do was shake his despondently. "Sir, Spears four and five are completely gone. Both paladins and horses." Lolark thought back to his encounter with the young paladin at Silver Cross Keep. Sir Benjamin would have been swept away by spear five. What an incredible waste of young talent. Sir Roderick paused to collect himself. "Spear three is down to one hundred seventeen paladins, although only about half still have their warhorses."

Lolark kept his face still. He dared not show his true emotions in front of the men. It would not be good for morale. Internally, however, Lolark was completely overcome by the devastation of the twister. "Sir Roderick, you are now known as Sir Roderick the Stout. Wear the name with honor. Report back to your spear and take command of spear three. Some of your men will have to complete the mission on foot."

"Yes, sir!" Sir Roderick saluted Lolark proudly and hustled back to the north on foot.

"Spear commanders," Lolark said, "Gather up your men and gear. We move out one hour."

Lolark observed the men of his phalanx slowly gather what was remaining of their belongings. This storm was a significant blow, and he knew the men would struggle to come to grips with its aftermath. The men needed a morale boost. He decided to address each of the spears. "Sir Oliver!" he called.

"Yes, Sir?" answered Oliver.

"I am riding to the remnants of the third spear. I will return shortly. Have your spear and and Sir Philip's spear assembled upon my return. I will address each of them in turn."

"Yes, sir!"

Lolark rode to the north to oversee the regrouping of spear three. As he rode, he lost himself in his thoughts. He wondered if he would be able to ever fully recover from such a loss. An uncontrollable force decimated nearly half of his phalanx in a matter of minutes. No amount of training could have prevented the loss. This one factor alone moved him closer to a decision to accept the quartermaster position. Lolark shook off the dark thoughts for now. He needed to re-instill the morale of his men to complete this mission.

Lolark arrived at the spear three encampment. He had thought that spears one and two appeared demoralized. What he witnessed here was astonishing. Half of the spear remained lying on the ground. Some men were crying out in pain. One hundred and seventeen may have survived the twister, but some were clearly grievously injured.

"Sir Roderick the Stout!" Lolark called out.

"Yes, sir!" a shout came back. Sir Roderick trotted up to Lolark.

"Do you have a report on the casualties?"

"Yes, Sir. One hundred seventeen paladins from spear three yet live. However, all are injured, some much worse than others."

"Have your men heal the worst of the injured. Make sure to heal any broken bones when possible. When you are completed with the healing, gather your gear and form up. I will address the spear."

"Yes, sir!" Roderick said with a salute. He then turned and began barking out commands. Lolark could see the paladins moving to heal some men. After nearly an hour of observing the men slowly pick themselves up, gather their gear, and form up, Lolark had a new sense of pride in these men he had trained. These men could overcome such an ordeal and carry on with their mission.

After the last of them formed up, Lolark sat tall atop his horse in front of the remnants of spear three. "Paladins of the Silver Cross," Lolark began in a calm, commanding voice, "you have a choice before you. Will you be defined by the adversity you face? Or would you rather be defined by how you react to that adversity? You have suffered tremendous loss here today, of that there is no doubt. However, we still have a mission to complete. The people of Westmoor are in need of our assistance. Will we leave them to the atrocities that the grendlaar will visit upon them? Or will we be the force that ensures that they continue to live long and prosperous lives? These are the stories that bards sing about for generations to come. Let us become the heroes of that story! For honor and life!"

"For honor and life!" the paladins shouted back.

Lolark returned to the south and addressed spears one and two individually with more or less the same speech. A full two hours after the storm, Lolark's phalanx of Silver Cross paladins continued on their mission, beleaguered but no longer demoralized. They *would* reach Westmoor and save the townspeople from the grendlaar.

As Lolark rode in the silence at the head of the phalanx with Oliver at his side. Oliver, sensing something odd with his friend's demeanor, asked, "A dolcot for your thoughts, Lolark."

Lolark continued to look to the south. He took in a long breath and exhaled slowly. "I've been wrestling with a decision, Oliver. You know that I've been offered the quartermaster position at Silver Cross Keep." Oliver nodded. "I'm tired of this endless fighting and the continual losses it creates. I think it may be time for me to move on to do something different." Oliver continued to listen in silence. "This disaster with the storm has made me consider it even more. We lost so many men in an instant. Many of those taken away by the storm were barely sixteen years old. I'm just tired, old friend, and wondering if it's all worth it."

"Lolark, you've made such a positive impact on the lives of so many paladins, mine included. You have done lots of good for the order. Surely, you want to focus on that, rather than circumstances beyond your control. I can certainly understand your struggle, but please just think of all the young lives you could continue to influence in the future as a phalanx commander and training officer."

Lolark paused for a moment, then said, "I appreciate your candor, Oliver. I will take your wise words into consideration."

Soon, the foothills gave way to full-sized hills. The phalanx had to move to half its width because of the change in terrain. The paladins no longer could ride at a trot anymore, either.

Lady Sophia rode up to Oliver and spoke to him briefly. "Lolark," Sir Oliver said, "it appears the storm came directly through the area just ahead of us. Look at all the destruction."

"Yes, I noticed that myself. But there's nothing to do but continue on."

As they moved closer to Westmoor, however, it was becoming apparent that they wouldn't be able to continue on their present course. "Look at that debris up ahead, Oliver,"

Lolark said.

"It looks like that twister dumped all the trees and other objects it picked up and dumped them in that pass ahead," replied Oliver.

"Let's get a little closer to see what the situation is," said Lolark. Oliver nodded in agreement.

As they neared the pass, however, their worst fears were realized. The pass was completely impassable. "Unfortunately, it looks like we'll have to turn around and find a different way," said Lolark.

"We'll be unable to perform a counter-column," said Sir Oliver. "There's not enough space between these hills."

"We'll have to perform a counter-march, and have the rear of the column take the lead, Oliver."

"But that will place the unmounted paladins at the head of the column! It will significantly slow our progress."

"It is what the Spirits have provided, Oliver. We'll back up until we can find a pass to the west and approach Westmoor from the plains. We probably won't get there before the grendlaar, though. Send a messenger down the line to inform them we need to perform a counter-march." Oliver called over Lady Sophia and gave the order.

Lolark turned Lion to face the first spear. "We are going to perform a counter-march. The way ahead is blocked," Lolark shouted to them. The paladins performed an about face and waited for the column to move again."

Before long, the column was moving to the north, but it was much slower than their passage southward. The force rode for another hour before they came to a stop. "Oliver, send a messenger again to find out what the delay is." Oliver again gave Lady Sophia the command, and she rode off to the north.

The column began moving again before the messenger returned. Upon his return, Lady Sophia immediately reported to Sir Oliver.

"Sir, the third spear found a pass to the west, but it is narrower than the one we are currently traveling on. They had to make an adjustment at the front of the column. We'll only be able to ride two-abreast through the pass."

"I don't like this," said Lolark. "We're getting choked through the pass."

"Well, we should be through the pass fairly quickly. We can't be too far from the western foothills," replied Oliver.

"We should be extra wary, just in case."

They continued to ride in silence until they came to the pass. It took some time to adjust the formation to fit to the narrower path, but they were on their way before too long. They traveled to the west for another thirty minutes, keeping watch all around to look for any signs of an ambush in the constricted pass.

"Oliver, stop. Do you see that movement at the base of the hills to the south?" Lolark pointed his gauntleted hand in that direction.

"Yes, I see it. It's ever so slight, but something is definitely there."

"Look to the north," Lolark instructed.

"Yes, I see some movement there, too."

"Men," Lolark called out, "prepare for an ambush from the hills on both sides of the pass."

The paladins immediately directed their mounts to the flanks to form lines on both the north and south sides. They drew their lances in anticipation of an attack. Within a matter of seconds, dozens of figures armed with spears erupted from the hills and charged towards the paladins. Grendlaar.

"Hold the line! Just a few more moments," Lolark commanded. "Charge!"

The line of paladins rode in formation towards the grendlaar with their lances pointed forward. It didn't take long for the paladins to reach the charging grendlaar. Many grendlaar ended up on the end of a lance. Once the initial attack had finished. Drawing their long swords, the paladins reacted immediately. The remaining grendlaar ferociously stabbed at the warriors and their mounts with their spears. With long slashing movements, the paladins responded with their swords.

A score of grendlaar surrounded Lolark and Oliver, who stood apart from the formation of paladins. Their horses stomped and bit at the grendlaar, but it was difficult for Lolark to get the horse close enough to the grendlaar for that to be effective. Lolark and Oliver were slashing at them with their long swords, felling many in the process. One grendlaar managed to get quite close to Lolark's left flank. He could see a spear thrust at him. Lolark used his sword to deflect the spear downwards. The grendlaar's spear continued moving forward, however, and slashed Lion on the side of his abdomen. The horse cried out in pain.

Lolark started sliding off Lion to his right, saddle and all. He wondered what had happened. Lolark crashed to the ground. Lion roared in anger as he moved to protect Lolark, who was prone on the ground. A dozen grendlaar began stabbing at Lolark as he lay on the ground. They were howling with glee. Lion crashed into them, stomping and biting, and forcing them away from Lolark. The brief respite was enough for Lolark to get up and get his bearings straight. He couldn't find his sword, which he had dropped when falling, so he grabbed his mace from the holster on Lion's saddle, which lay next to him.

Lolark took a moment to survey the battlefield. From his vantage point on the ground, he couldn't see much toward the front of the column. The flanks of the first spear, however, appeared to be handling the battle capably. Scores of dead grendlaar were lying at the hooves of the warhorses. Lolark and Lion fought side-by-side. Lion was ferociously stomping on grendlaar as they approached. The ones who could get through Lion's hooves were met with his teeth as he tore flesh from their bodies with his powerful bites. At the same time, Lolark swung his mace savagely, cracking skulls and breaking legs.

Before long, the battle began to slow down. Some remaining grendlaar retreated to the hills. Lolark looked around for Sir Oliver. Catching sight of him to the northwest, he called for him. Oliver immediately rode over to Lolark.

"Lolark, are you alright? I saw you fall from your horse."

"Yes. My armor is pretty banged up, but I'm uninjured."

Lolark turned to Lion and gently stroked the side of his neck. "You've been an excellent soldier, Lion. You deserve some adamons when we get back to Silver Cross Keep." Lolark noticed a deep cut along Lion's left flank. Lolark laid his hands on Lion's wound and softly spoke a prayer as he applied fauna and water spirits to the wound. Lion's wound slowly knit itself back together. Lolark turned to Oliver. "What happened to my saddle?" They both approached the saddle lying on the ground. "Look, Oliver. The girth strap must have been cut with the spear thrust that injured Lion."

"What an unfortunate stroke of luck," Oliver said.

"We'll need to find a replacement for the girth strap so that I can continue to ride to Westmoor."

"That shouldn't be a problem, sir," replied Oliver.

"What are our casualties?"

"Ten dead and three injured," replied Oliver. "But we lost no horses."

"And the grendlaar?"

"We estimate about one hundred dead on the ground. A few dozen escaped into the hills."

"I'd say that's quite a success—a ten to one kill ratio. You've trained these youngsters well, Oliver."

"Thank you, Sir. But the grendlaar's strength has always been in numbers. They didn't have that many here to cause much of a problem."

Lolark nodded. "What of the other spears?"

"They're still ahead of us. It was over before they could do much for us."

"Well, muster the spear and let's move out."

"Yes, sir." Oliver turned to his spear and shouted the commands to form up. Before long they could continue their movement west. They had salvaged a girth strap from one of the warhorse's whose paladin had been slain and got Lolark riding on Lion again.

About an hour later, the rear of the column emerged from the hills onto the plains to the west. The town of Westmoor could be seen in the distance to the south.

"Oliver," Lolark called out, "let's reform the phalanx to ten wide with first spear at the head.

"Yes, sir." Oliver began giving commands to his banner leaders and sent off a messenger to the other spears.

Once the phalanx was back in formation, they headed toward Westmoor. Within an hour, it got dark. "Oliver, send the word that we are going to set up camp for the night. After our harrowing experiences today, the men could use some rest."

"With all due respect, sir, I think we should continue on. The grendlaar may have already taken the town. If we stop to rest, we may arrive at a ghost town tomorrow. We owe it to the townspeople to get there as soon as we can and save as many people as possible."

"But the men-" Lolark began.

"Are ready for this, sir. We can do it!"

"Very well. You've convinced me, Oliver. We continue on."

It took another hour to reach the outskirts of Westmoor. They were unprepared for what they witnessed. The town of Westmoor looked to be surrounded by thousands of grendlaar. And that was just what they could see from the north side. The estimate of five thousand might have been low. At least they hadn't overrun the town yet.

"Orders, sir?" Oliver asked Lolark.

"You were wise in your assessment, Oliver. We were able to arrive before the grendlaar could get inside the town. However, I believe an attack now would be ill advised since the grendlaar can see in the dark much better than we can. We will redeploy the phalanx to a full front, rather than column formation. We will then rest in shifts, by spear, until morning. One spear will be alert at all times. If it looks like the grendlaar are breaching the walls, we will end our rest and immediately attack."

"Yes, sir." Oliver again relayed the commands to Lady Sophia.

The phalanx formed up in a full front formation. Once in position, the rest rotation began.

৩৽৵

The night passed without incident. The phalanx mustered into a battle-ready formation. Lolark rode to the front and center of the entire phalanx. He cast a minor spell to amplify his voice so that the entire phalanx could hear him.

"This is it, lads!" Lolark called out. "Your chance to show your battle readiness. This is the mission of the paladin orders-to defend the innocent. Your spear commanders have your orders. You ride forth today for honor and life!"

"For honor and life!" the chorus of paladins echoed back to Lolark.

Lolark turned Lion to look at the town of Westmoor and the future battlefield. His phalanx was ready for this. He believed it. Once the spear commanders had time to deliver the orders to their troops, Lolark turned to see nearly five hundred paladins with lances at the ready.

"Charge!" he commanded.

The entire phalanx moved as one, charging the mass of grendlaar before them. The sound of horses' hooves crashing on the ground overpowered the paladins' shouts. With spears thrust forward, the grendlaar horde turned to face the oncoming paladins. The front of the phalanx smashed into the grendlaar, killing hundreds in the first attack. The paladins immediately dropped their broken lances and drew their long swords to continue the attack.

Several horns suddenly rang out. Lolark wondered who blew the horns. It didn't take long for him to realize it wasn't allies. He could see thousands more grendlaar pouring from the east and west sides of Westmoor's wooden palisade. They just kept coming. Soon, upwards of ten thousand grendlaar would surround his phalanx.

"Form a square!" Lolark shouted with his still amplified voice. Squares were normally used to defend against cavalry, but they could also be used to avoid being surrounded by an enemy. His phalanx' training proved effective because they quickly reformed the entire phalanx into a square. Now it would be a battle of attrition. Lolark wasn't sure if he had the numbers to survive a battle of attrition, but he and his men would die trying. From the center of the square, Lolark could see the paladins killing grendlaar by the dozens, but his own men were also dying. The square continued to get smaller as more of his men fell. It certainly didn't look as if the numbers favored the Silver Cross Keep paladins today.

Lolark looked to all sides of the square. There must be something to do to avoid a complete slaughter. Then he saw it. It was a slim opportunity, but it was there. The grendlaar numbers on the northern flank were much smaller than on the other three flanks. "Men on the east, west, and south flanks!" Lolark shouted out. "The rear two ranks peel off, form a boar's tooth and drive it through the north flank. The front two ranks, hold the grendlaar back with everything you have!"

The paladins immediately carried out Lolark's commands. The paladins on the northern flank made an opening for the boar's tooth to strike through to the grendlaar horde. The initial strike was remarkably successful. It scattered the grendlaar to the sides. The mounted paladins of the spearhead turned around

after the initial strike to regroup for another attack from the north. Lolark noticed something behind the regrouping paladins. It was a group of at least one
hundred armored men marching in formation to the battle. Lolark tried to think
of who it could be when he saw a banner flying in front of the formation. A
silver cross on a blue background! Some men must have survived the tornado,
and they must have marched all night to get here.

Lolark turned back to the rest of the phalanx. "Paladins of the Silver
Cross," he called with his enhanced voice, "make a strategic retreat and reform
with the men at the northern flank." The paladins of the Silver Cross executed
this maneuver with precision. The paladins of the boar's head, the northern
flank, and the newly arrived paladins quickly dispatched the smaller force of
grendlaar in the north.

Lolark rode ahead to greet the paladins who had just arrived. As he
rode up to them, he could see that they had been to hell and back. Their armor
showed heavy damage. Many of them were missing pieces of armor. None of
them wore helms. All of them had cuts and bruises on their faces and heads.
As he was looking out over their formation, he noticed one figure who looked
familiar. Sir Benjamin! Lolark's heart buoyed at the sudden discovery. Sir Benjamin returned a confident grin to Lolark.

The remaining paladins of the phalanx formed a battle front to face
the grendlaar. It was approximately five hundred paladins, some of them on
horseback and some on foot, against thousands of grendlaar. Lolark sat high
in his saddle and called out, "Let us write a bard song that will live for the ages!
For life and honor!"

"For life and honor!" the paladins called back. The Silver Cross paladins bravely faced off against the grendlaar horde. They screamed and brutally
unleashed their attacks on the grendlaar.

Then, more horns sounded out in the battle's cacophony. *By the Spirits,*
Lolark thought. *Are there even more grendlaar coming?* Then he saw it. More than
a thousand knights on horseback charging from the south. At the front of the
phalanx of knights, a rider carried a banner bearing the coat of arms of the

knights of Blue Keep, golden swords crossed on a royal blue background. They pounded into the rear of the grendlaar. This immediately caused the grendlaar to erupt into a panic. With mounted soldiers on both sides, the grendlaar didn't know which way to go. Lolark's own paladins, energized by the appearance of the knights, redoubled their efforts and began to push the grendlaar back.

The knights of Blue Keep began to fan out to encompass the grendlaar on all sides. The knights became the hammer and the paladins the anvil as the grendlaar were being pounded in the middle. After what seemed an eternity, the battle was over. Most of the grendlaar lay dead in the plains outside of Westmoor. Several hundred, however, escaped into the hills to the northwest. Lolark had his realization then and there. Oliver was right. He could still accomplish much good as a phalanx commander. He would decline the quartermaster position and continue to mentor young paladins in the order.

A lone knight approached Lolark on horseback. "Well met, good knight!" called Lolark.

The knight held out his hand to Lolark, who grasped the knights' wrist, and they shook.

"I am Sir Michael of the knights of Blue Keep."

"Sir Michael the Timely, you mean. I am Sir Lolark the Valiant of the Silver Cross paladins."

Oliver rode up beside Lolark. "After this campaign, we'll have to call you Sir Lolark the unlucky," Oliver said wryly.

"Your assistance is much appreciated, Sir Michael," said Lolark.

"It was our pleasure, Sir Lolark. We would have been here sooner, but our intelligence reported that a force of five thousand grendlaar was descending upon Cairthorn. When we learned our report was in error, we returned immediately at double time."

"Our reports indicated that five thousand grendlaar were on their way to assault Westmoor. It appears that Cairthorn may have been a feint to enable them to do a massive assault on Westmoor," said Lolark.

Sir Michael nodded in agreement. "Sir Lolark, may we offer you some respite at the Blue Keep?"

"That would be welcome indeed, Sir Michael. May we repay your timeliness by offering healing to your men?"

"I will not say no to such a generous offer, Sir Lolark. Now, let us clean up the battlefield and travel to Blue Keep for some merriment and stories, my friend."

"I look forward to the stories we will share, my friend."

The End

# ERICH THE BLACK
by
Daniel E. Myers

The morning was crisp and chilly for Cairthorn this time of year. Erich lifted the collar of his overcoat as he turned the corner and almost ran into three guardsmen surrounding a body on the ground. "What happened here?" he asked.

"Attacked by wild dogs." The captain of the guard proclaimed. "Note the bite marks, and the partially eaten thighs and hips."

Indeed, the woman, a Black Aelf who looked remarkably like the Black Aelf priest who had raised Erich, had numerous bite marks on her legs and hips. The noble woman, if the velvet and jeweled necklace was any indication, had been partially devoured. But Erich doubted it was wild dogs, or animals of any kind, which had killed her. "Who is she?" Erich asked.

"I have no idea," he answered. "Some aelf, by the looks of her."

The fact that the captain did not know who she was, despite her obvious status, raised Erich's suspicions immediately. "May I?" Erich asked the captain.

"Who are you?" the captain asked suspiciously.

"Just a priest from the Black Woods, visiting this fine city." Erich replied. Displaying the small silver oak tree on the chain he wore around his neck.

"Very well," the captain conceded. "Let me know what you find."

Erich didn't really hold any enmity towards the captain. His job was to ensure order, but his skill was not finding causes of death. Erich examined the body carefully. In the back of her head he found the remains of a needle embedded in the skull bone, likely from a blow dart. He made a mental note of the location. It would not be good to pull out his toolkit in front of the captain. He inspected the lips of the victim, along with her eyes. Neither indicated any discoloration or excessive bleeding.

He looked at the bite wounds next. There was no question that they were dog bites. Many dogs of different sizes as well. He noted there were no wounds on her hands or arms, though. This supported his just-formed theory that the woman had been incapacitated before the dogs attacked.

Erich looked up at the captain, "Do you mind if I bring her to my lab to preserve her body for the trip back to the Black Woods?" Erich caught a glimpse of movement behind the captain but noticed nothing when he changed his focus.

The captain almost let out a sign of relief. Nodding, he relaxed visibly. Erich could guess that the captain's prior dealings with Black Aelf, particularly when a crime had been committed against them, had not gone well. Their hatred of humans appeared to be inherent in their physical makeup. A thousand years of peace had not dulled their anger over the damage the humans had done to their woods.

Erich rode back to the tavern he was staying in and entered confidently. Walking over to the barkeep, he asked, "Any chance you have a wagon and draft horse I could make use of?"

Erich grinned as the barkeep looked him up and down. The fact that he had paid for the entire top floor would either reduce his price if the barkeep wanted to keep a good customer happy or increase it if the barkeep thought he could fleece a big spender out of even more silver. The barkeep went down the fleecing path. "Ten malnots if you get it returned before the blacksmith leaves, fifteen if I have to send for him later."

Erich counted out the ten malnots and set them on the counter. He made a mental note to make sure he liberated at least that much from the barkeep's coffers before he left. Erich turned towards the door and walked back the way he had come. He headed to the stables once outside and was surprised to see the tavern owner already there. Within minutes, he was on his way back to the dead aelf.

⚓

Captain Ferdinand Ramos was second guessing himself as he waited for the priest to return. Having a holy symbol didn't actually mean the man was a priest, although there were strong repercussions for those impersonating one. But a human priest from the Black Woods? That was unlikely. He had not even gotten the priest's name so he could send someone to check.

Two more guardsmen arrived, and Ferdinand debated with himself whether to have them haul the body to the morgue. Of course, that was at the local temple, which is where he assumed the priest would take it. "There is a priest coming by to pick up the body. You two stay with it until it gets to the morgue. Also, get the name of the priest and find out what he's doing in town."

Ferdinand wished he could stay and interrogate the priest himself. There was something about him that set the guard captain on edge. Nothing the man had done, but just the way he carried himself. Like the way he avoided giving his name, or the jet-black stallion he rode. He also didn't dress very priest-like, with a dark cloak and black riding boots over his dark gray shirt. Ferdinand had dealt with enough members of the Thieves' Guild to recognize the signs.

Bending over the body, he looked at it more closely. A youngish aelf by the looks of her. If she had been a human, he would have guessed she was in her early thirties. What that meant for an aelf was anyone's guess, but his was that she was between three and four hundred years old. Her clothing was exquisitely made, and there were no signs of a struggle. No bruises or anything to indicate she was attacked prior to the dogs devouring her. Likewise, the blood pools and stains matched the location of the wounds exactly.

Black Aelf were not unheard of in Cairthorn, but they were not common either. They also usually travelled in groups, unless they were doing something they didn't want everyone to be aware of. He got up and began walking back to the barracks. Baron Richie would want a report, particularly if the Black Aelf were involved. Shaking his head, he left muttering about his unfortunate lot in life.

❧

Erich was nearly sure that blue-seed poison had been used. A favorite among the vreen, it was made by crushing and boiling the seeds of several plants, most notably the wide bladed spear grass which grew in abundance in the vreen lands. Once most of the liquid cooled, bluish drops began forming, which were then filtered out and collected. The gelatinous beads could then be heated anytime and applied to weapons or used in darts. It was rumored some Vreen ate them in small amounts to help them sleep, but Erich had never heard of anyone else trying it.

The only problem was that blue-seed poison left a tell-tale blue mark on the skin around the wound. As he carefully examined the needle puncture on her neck, he could find no discoloration. He made a small incision to inspect the bone, but there was nothing to indicate blue-seed poison was used. It was strange, because if he wanted to kill someone in this fashion, it was the logical choice. But he had not studied poisons as diligently as he had other skills when he was part of the Thieves' Guild.

It wasn't that he was against killing people, but he had never dreamed of being an assassin, which was the main purpose of learning the poisons. Neither did he intend on becoming an inquisitor, where that knowledge would also be important. He merely wished to be a priest, but a priest who could live a lot better than the donations of a temple would support. And he found his priestly skills exquisitely complimented the skills he had learned in the guild. Particularly his skill at "walking the aether" as it was referred to in the temple.

Not knowing what else to do, he completed the autopsy, examining the body for signs of a struggle. He looked for bruising on the arms and around the neck, but in every aspect other than her partially eaten upper legs and buttocks, she looked to be perfectly healthy. Lastly, he plucked several strands of hair and placed them in a glass vial and corked it. *I will bring these to Robin, he will know what to look for,* He thought to himself.

He had met Robin years ago in the Black Woods when they were both young orphans under the care of Black Aelf. But Robin had run away from his abusive stepparents, and Erich had not seen him for years. Then, ten years ago, shortly after he had left the priesthood, he met Robin again in Voldair. They rekindled their old friendship immediately.

Robin had become a ward of the Thieves Guild in Voldair after leaving the Black Woods. Eventually, he joined the guild. After a month of pestering, Erich agreed to go with him to some guild meetings. A few months later, Erich joined as well. Robin had taken the assassin track and tried to get Erich to join him. But Erich joined just to learn some of the skills he thought would come in handy. Besides the common training on stealth and sleight of hand, he also studied lock picking and confidence scams, while Robin studied various poisons, drugs, and chemicals with a variety of effects.

Robin would know if it was poison, but Erich did not want to travel to Voldair. There was too much pressure for him to remain and teach the guild-masters some of his secrets. What was the point in being able to do things no one else could do if they made you show everyone how they were done? Besides, what he knew took twenty years of study in the temple to learn, none of the guild members could ever learn them. Not that the masters cared, they would force him to stay, nonetheless. So he sent a message through the guild.

§◦§

Surprisingly, Robin showed up the next day. "That was fast," Erich commented when Robin walked up. "You must have used a portal to get here."

"I am on my way to Northmoor. It seems some bandits have taken up residence there without paying their dues to the guild." Robin smiled and shrugged his shoulders. "The last emissary the guild sent has apparently joined them, so they sent me."

Erich smiled. It wasn't uncommon for independent guilds to form in these small towns, far from the oversight of the guild or a regent. But Northmoor was just outside the Southern Kingdom. Erich doubted the paladins at Silver Cross Keep or Gold Keep would appreciate bandits waylaying travelers.

"Why not send one of the orders after them?" Erich asked. "After all, it is their job to keep the roads clear."

"If the bandits refuse to join the guild, I have a small bag of turots for the knights at Blue Keep, to make them leave."

"Blue Keep?" Erich asked. "That's a bit far, and all the way south of the moors. Why not Gold Keep or Silver Cross Keep?"

Robin smiled. "The guild is currently out of sorts with the Palladium Council. Seems someone took a contract out on Sir Franklin the Fat. Sir Franklin detected the assassin who took the job, and the killing didn't go so well. Out of frustration, they mutilated the body, and carved runes on his belly. Now the council has declared that any guild members may be interrogated until the assassin is found."

"Who would take a contract to kill the leader of the council?" Erich asked. "Wait, it wasn't you, was it?"

"Oh no! Not me," Robin laughed while raising his hands. "I may be reckless sometimes, but I have no desire to have every paladin south of The Great Chasm hunting me. Especially that hill giant you hang out with occasionally."

"Besides the fact that giants are a myth, Lolark is not even the tallest human I have met."

"But were the other humans built like a castle tower?"

Erich scoffed. Lolark was big, and fierce in battle, but Erich had never met a more noble paladin. Instead of continuing the banter, Erich decided to get down to business. "Have you heard of a poison which mimics blue-seed poison, but doesn't stain the flesh?"

Robin thought a while. "I have, but they are quite rare. One is only found in the barbarian lands to the west, and only used by a certain tribe. The rest are difficult to make, and less reliable than blue-seed poison." Why do you ask?

"I decided to take on a bit of an inquisitor role for the local guard captain, and I suspect that blue seed was used, but there is no discoloration. No bleeding in the eyes or ears either, so I ruled out a number of other poisons." Erich held up the vial of hair for Robin. "I grabbed a sample of her hair. Would you be able to detect if it was something which built up in her system? I am thinking the dart may have just been a catalyst."

"Smart man," Robin said as he took the vial. "A couple of things come to mind. I will have to wait until I get back to do the analysis, though. Perhaps you would like to help me with my task, then I can help you with yours?"

"As long as the guild doesn't try to use this as a reason to force me back, I will. Besides, I hear rumors that the Vreen are starting to build armies again. I prefer to remain up above their usual raiding lands.

Robin laughed. "I doubt anyone in the guild wants you anywhere near Voldair after you left the last time. And I will draw up a contract so it is clear I hired you. You can just return the turots I pay you after I help you with your dilemma. As for the Vreen, they seem to do this every twenty years or so, and they are always defeated. I wouldn't worry too much about them."

Two days later, Erich and Robin found themselves surrounded by over forty men on a land-bridge between two patches of swamp. Half were on horseback, several wearing heavier armor than most guild members preferred.

"Halt, this road is protected by the Warriors of the Moor. We apologize, but we must ask for a road fee to pay for our protection of these roads. Just two turots each. Quite reasonable I think you will agree."

"Of course," Robin pulled out his purse, and his guild totem as he spoke. "Just show me your totem from Voldair and I will hand you the money."

The armored brute in front of him paled, but quickly gained his composure. "These are not Voldair lands, and we do not recognize their totem. We pay our due to the Moor Guild."

Robin looked at Erich and laughed. Erich smiled back. Robin put his purse back inside his cloak and held the token for all the bandits to see. "I see. But I have never heard of the Moor Guild, are you saying you exist outside the oversight of the guild masters in Voldair?"

A weasel faced man spoke up. "I know you, Robin, and you would be better off joining us. Perhaps your friend Erich would like to join us and survive to see tomorrow."

"Don't bring me into this, Alexander. I merely came here to keep my friend company. Don't confuse me with an honorless knave who turns on his masters for a bit of gold. And I do *not* like to be threatened."

"So, you know my name. Did you think that would intimidate me? We will see you join us or die."

Robin laughed. "Who do you think you are talking to? Do we look like mere messengers, sent to present a warning to some miscreants? We are here to demand you pay your dues to the Guild or face the consequences. I think a thousand havnots would suffice for your initiation fee."

Erich looked at Robin. It was clear he was spoiling for a fight, and Erich was not looking forward to odds of a score to one. He looked over at his friend.

Robin smiled. Then he turned back to the man blocking their path. "I have given you your options. Do you wish to pay the initiation, or face the wrath of the guild?"

"I think we shall just kill you both and send your heads to the guild as our initiation fee."

Then the brigands charged, while the remaining brigands loosed a score of arrows. Robin turned his horse to flee, as Erich summoned spirits to do his bidding. In seconds, Erich's horse, Challenger, was riding off without him as a dense fog obscured the area. A few seconds later, Alexander found himself plummeting to the ground as his horse's front leg was severed above the knee.

This stopped the charge.

"Find the guild's lackeys," Alexander screamed from underneath his fallen horse.

"I would stay down if I were you." Erich knew Alexander would recognize his dulcet tones. "Better to face the guild's justice tomorrow than my blade today."

"Erich is over here," were the last words Alexander spoke before Erich's rapier sliced his throat cleanly through.

Erich rose and disappeared once more into the fog. The bowmen, his horse limping, but staying near had brought Robin down. But Robin had turned the men behind him, giving Erich a score of targets. He wasted no time in sneaking up on them one by one, the unnatural fog cloaking him until it was too late. He was halfway through the brigands who had been behind them when the fog began lifting.

Erich dispatched two more, then whistled for Challenger, who charged back through the brigands. Erich used the distraction to eliminate another one of the thieves "guarding" the moors. Robin was less productive, maintaining a purely defensive posture. Outnumbered four to one, Robin fought bravely, disabling two of the attackers with gut wounds before he received a gut wound of his own. Erich charged Challenger through the two remaining brigands before they could finish Robin off, kicking one to the ground after skewering the other through his chainmail.

Both Erich and Robin had wounds. Erich's were not life threatening, but Robin would bleed out if he wasn't attended to soon. Erich jumped down as the other thieves cautiously approached them. After helping Robin onto his horse and breaking the arrow protruding from its shoulder, he mounted Challenger and the two friends rode off, arrows peppering the ground they had just been holding.

"Well done, my friend," Robin said with a big grin.

"It would have been better if we had not had to engage them at all," Erich scolded. "You are too reckless, my friend."

The bandits across the land-bridge began moving cautiously towards them. Robin began moving his hands, and sent three silver lights into the lead thug, causing him to falter. Erich looked at his younger friend. "When did you start studying the spirits?"

"About a year ago. I met one of the members of the Red Crest Magistry. He began teaching me air cantrips and said I had a knack for it. I learned a few spells, like this one."

Robin waved his hands again, and a ribbon of fire leaped from his hands, halting the charging outlaws as they dove out of the way. Once again, the lead thug was caught full in the chest. His screams were mercifully short as his cloak burst into flames. Robin turned and rode away, slumping in the saddle. Erich was right beside him, and in minutes they had left the remaining bandits licking their wounds.

Robin reached into a pouch hidden in his cloak, pulling out a small bag with herbs.

"Allow me, my friend." Erich's hand began glowing, and he pressed it against Robins wound.

Robin smiled as the wound stopped bleeding. "Couldn't you have given me a little more of the spirit?" he asked. "I thought you were a mighty priest."

"High Priest, to be exact." Erich smiled back. "But if I were to give you more, you would remain just as reckless. Perhaps the open wound will serve to remind you that it is just the two of us."

"Well then, let's get to Blue Keep. Then we can report back to Voldair."

"I am not returning to Voldair. You will have to report without me."

"Hahahahahahaha. I forgot about that incident with the Guild Master's wife."

"It is not my fault women find me irresistible. Besides, she never told me she was married, and I had just gone through my annual tithing." Erich sent Robin a look that the conversation was over, and Robin laughed again.

A few hours later, after resting and Robin using a poultice to cover and treat his wound, they headed to Blue Keep, Robin riding on a makeshift litter Erich had made out of an abandoned wagon. The trip was uneventful and they arrived at Blue Keep the next day. Robin handed out the bag of turots to the keep's commander to keep the road clear. Erich had no doubt they would find more brigands after yesterday's encounter.

৵৵

Two days later they were back in Erich's room.

They tested the hair meticulously for any signs of chemicals or drugs being imbibed by the victim prior to the killing but found nothing. "I guess we can rule out a catalyst then," Erich said with a scowl.

"You were right on the other part though. It does resemble blue-seed poison," Robin told him. "It appears they have refined it, distilling the poison out while leaving the seed oil behind."

"But I thought it was the oil which was the poison."

"Many do, but in reality, it is contained in the meat of the seed. That is why they dry it and grind it then mix it with alcohol. It isn't soluble in oil or water." Robin pointed at a barely visible piece of curdled flesh near the incision. "This is strange. What do you make of it?"

Erich looked through the large magnifying glass at the wound again. Robin was correct, there was a small piece of skin near a capillary that looked like it had been caused by some sort of acid. Congealed blood was almost encasing it, which is why he hadn't noticed it earlier. He thought hard. *Was there a reason the assassin would tip the dart with acid?* He could think of no reason. "I give up. Other than adding acid to the dart, I cannot explain it. But I also cannot explain why anyone would do that.

"They didn't. I think the dart hit the blood vessel, and for some reason reacted with her blood, creating the acid. But blue-seed poison doesn't do that. Of course, if they refined it, I am not really sure what the effect would be." Robin took another look, then turned to Erich. "We should stop for the day, and I will get some blue-seed poison and see if we can recreate this."

"That sounds like a great idea," Erich agreed. I think you owe me dinner anyway after getting me shot and nearly chopped up."

An hour later they were in the Tortoise Palace, sitting at a tiny round table holding a plate stacked high with fruit and cheeses. Erich started the conversation. "So tell me about your study of the spirits. What have you learned so far?"

"Just the basics. How to send my aura into the aether and gather the spirits. And then how to weave some of them together. I am pretty good with air and fire and aether, but water and earth evade me."

Erich laughed. "What about wood, and flora and fauna and stone and seawater?"

Robin scowled at his friend. "I am not studying to be a priest." Robin picked up a piece of cheese and held it out to Erich. "Can a priest do this?" The piece of cheese shuddered then melted, dripping on Erich's side of the plate.

"But of course," Erich replied. He then picked up a piece of cheese of his own and it became encased in flame, melting in the palm of his hand. Once the flame was out, he poured the melted cheese out onto Robin's side of the plate. He then showed Robin his spotless hand.

"That is impressive. I didn't know priests did spells like that."

"Just a cantrip, like yours," Erich replied. "Priests must master all the spirits. We just prefer to use our abilities to grow and nurture rather than destroy. Mages used the elemental spirits because back when the elemental worlds invaded our world, there was much more power in them."

"Yes," Robin replied. "He did mention that. But he made it sound like priests could do little more than start campfires or sweep water from a brook into a bucket."

Erich laughed. "Go to Golden Chalice Keep and talk to the war priests there. You will find they are as adept with the elemental spirits as anyone. More so, I dare say. I studied there for two years and it opened my eyes greatly. I even learned a trick which I am told only a handful of priests have mastered. And as far as I know, no mage is even aware of its possibility."

Robin nodded thoughtfully. "OK," he said. "What is it, if I may ask?"

"You may not," Erich said, but with a gentle tone. "It is a valuable skill, made more valuable by its secrecy. I would not betray my fellow priests by revealing its nature. But I will make this promise. I will teach you if I ever feel you have reached the skill with the spirits to master it."

"Deal!" Robin said as his eyes lit up. But Erich knew he would likely never teach Robin the skill. It was not meant for someone so reckless.

Their conversation was interrupted as a princess approached the table and leaned over to them and said with a quiet and husky voice, "Master John would ask that you limit your displays of spirit use, please. Perhaps you would care to engage in some other activity instead of your mage duels?"

Both men laughed, and each of them slid a turot over to the young princess. "Perhaps you can find a friend to join us. To keep us in line of course."

"Of course," she said with a melodious giggle. "But be advised, we have many ways of administering punishment to those who deserve it."

Erich laughed again. "Are you trying to prevent us from misbehaving or encouraging us."

The princess giggled again and left, returning shortly with another similarly attired young women, and the four talked and drank until the evening was over.

They started the next day trying different ways to create blue-seed poison and refine it. Nothing worked. Each time they attempted to distill the blue droplets, they ended up with a whitish substance that turned hard and precipitated out of solution as soon as it cooled. After several hours with no success, they sat back to discuss the problem.

"Maybe it is the alcohol that is the problem," Erich said. "Can we try something made from honey, or fruit instead of grain?"

"That is a good idea," Robin admitted. "I will go to the inn and see what kinds I can gather."

Erich called after him, "Maybe we should focus on something made in the Vreen lands."

"Another good idea," Robin called back as he mounted his horse. Then he rode off to the inn.

Robin wasn't gone for more than a half hour, during which Erich took a quick break to fix a small lunch. Bread and hard salami, which he knew Robin favored. He favored it too, once he had been introduced to it at a tavern in Foresight, capital of the Middle Kingdom. He forgot the name of the place, but it seemed to have access to foods no one else could obtain. Perhaps it was because the deposed queen of the Southern Kingdom ran it.

Whatever the case, it was delicious. Paired with some cheeses imported from across the dwarven and northern kingdoms, and some warm slices of lamb and seared venison backstrap, it would be a sumptuous lunch. It was good to have the resources of a life well spent in the service of the spirits, and himself of course.

Robin returned and after lunch, they tried the various alcohols to no avail. Erich sat back dejectedly. "So we don't know why they used acid, and we can't figure out how they refined the oil out," he said. "You are the expert, is there anything else we are missing?"

"No," Robin replied. "It makes no sense. They must have figured out some way to refine it, but it may even be a combination of things. And still we have the question of the acid."

"Maybe that's it," Erich exclaimed. "Maybe they don't dissolve it in alcohol, maybe they require the acid to keep it in suspension."

Sure enough, after drying and scraping the precipitate into a vial, they added some spit from a swamp dragon. There were better acids, but Erich just happened to have some in his lab. They sealed the vial and shook it, and the clear liquid seemed to indicate their success.

"Now we just need to figure out who else knows how to do this."

"I had an instructor in Voldair who talked about this," Robin offered. "Other than him, I don't know who could do this. And he died several months ago."

"Someone else from Voldair, then?" Erich asked.

"I have not heard of anyone else in Voldair even discussing this. It seems unlikely that it was commonly done. There are so many easier ways to poison someone."

A knock at the door interrupted their discussion. "Are you expecting anyone?" Robin asked.

"I am not. Let's see who it is."

Erich led the way out of the lab, then paused and closed the doors behind Robin. They went through the parlor and into the front hall, where the banging on the door was increasing in tempo and force.

Erich pulled the doors open quickly, and two guardsmen nearly fell through. Behind them, none other than the mayor and the remainder of a squad of guards stood. But Erich ignored them and focused on a lone Black Aelf who stood just behind the mayor.

"Erich the Black, I presume?" the mayor said, looking Erich in the eye.

"I am," Erich said simply. "To what do I owe the honor for this exalted audience?"

"We would like to talk to you about the aelf you are currently performing your experiments on."

"I am investigating the manner of her death, not experimenting." Erich scowled, then gave a small bow. "As a former denizen of the Black Woods, I felt an obligation to find the truth of her death."

"This is General Sannoval an Assai, and he believes the woman is his wife. He would like to identify the body before she decomposes beyond recognition."

"I assure you, General, I have already performed the rituals to preserve the body. You will find her in the same condition I did. Please come in."

"No!" the mayor nearly barked. "We will transport the body to the nearest temple ourselves. You men, search the house and bring the body to the temple."

"I am happy to show you where she is, Lord Richie," Erich offered.

"That will not be needed. I know who you and your companion are, and we are taking you into custody as well. We have questions as to why two members of the Thieves' Guild took such a sudden interest into the death of a Black Aelf."

"I assure you," Erich began before being cut off by the Baron.

"I need no assurances from you. You may follow us, or I will send my knights to fetch you."

Erich looked over at Robin, noticing his fingers flashing. A small shake of his head, and the fingers stopped. "We will be happy to accompany you and answer any questions you may have."

The walk through the city was a pleasant one, despite the gruff attitude of the mayor, and the constant shoving by the guardsmen. Robin had wanted to make a run for it, but Erich had intentions of staying here in Cairthorn and was willing to put up with a little jostling to keep the peace. He was a bit surprised though when they were placed in cells and left alone.

✎

Late that night, Erich was awakened by Robin. "Let's get out of here. The security is so lax, I didn't even need to subdue any guards to get out of my cell."

"This isn't their dungeon. These are holding cells, until they are ready to interrogate us. Go back to your cell and be patient. We have done nothing wrong, and they will soon find out we did nothing wrong."

"Easy for you to say. I am due back in Voldair." Robin shook his head. "If I don't report back, they might think I joined the brigands and put a contract out on me, like the one on Alexander."

Erich grinned in understanding. "So that is why you wanted to confront them first. Were you planning on telling me about it?"

"No," Robin admitted. "I had several contracts to execute, that one was actually the smallest. I will send the proceeds, less my commission, once I receive them."

"Make sure you do," Erich said with a wide grin. "I would hate our friendship to end over a paltry sum of turots. And I would miss our conversations."

Robin laughed at the not-so-veiled threat. He was pretty sure Erich was joking but made a mental note to send the turots to him once he collected. He got up and left Erich's cell, giving Erich one last chance before relocking the door.

✎

The next morning an inquisitor came for Robin and brought him into a brightly lit room, with a scribe sitting in the corner. "I am Sir Fits-William," the inquisitor introduced himself. "I have some questions for you."

"So I am told," Robin replied, his face relaxed in a mask of cold indifference. "Ask away then."

Sir Fits-William stood over him, towering and intimidating, but Robin's calm demeanor seemed to make him bristle.

"You were seen at the Plum House the night Lord Slovak was murdered. Let me guess—you were just passing the time?"

"I doubt it was me. I came though the western gate and went straight to my friend's home to recruit him for a task and help him with one. I have not been near the Plum House. Besides, I prefer the Tortoise Palace."

Sir Fits-William leaned closer, his voice low and threatening. "A convenient answer. But someone saw you. A hooded figure. Your height. Your build."

Robin shrugged slightly. "Hoods are common. So are people of my stature."

"But most people aren't members of the assassins' guild. And they don't leave corpses in their wake. This dagger," he placed the bloodied blade on the table between them "is foreign. Made by a smith in Voldair. A professional's weapon. You'd know something about that, wouldn't you?"

Robin glanced at the dagger but showed no emotion. "I've never seen it before."

Sir Fits-William tapped the blade with a finger, his tone mocking. "And the man you travel with? Erich the Black. What's his part in this? Your accomplice?"

Robin leaned back slightly, his voice cool, "Erich? He is a well-respected priest of the Forest Spirits. He used to be High Priest of the Black Woods Shrine. You can't possibly think he would have anything to do with killing people."

Sir Fits-William studied Robin's face. "A priest you say. I have it on good authority that he spent several years training in the Thieves' Guild. In Voldair, no less. Probably where you met him."

"No actually. I did help him get into the guild though. But he left to seek his fortune while I studied. We don't get together often, but we try to get together at least every couple of years. He actually sent for me to assist him with the investigation in the death of the aelf woman. Look, here is his letter to me."

Sir Fits-William read the letter. "So I am to believe that is why you are in Cairthorn too? A little convenient, don't you think?"

"Convenient for whom?" Robin asked. "Not me. I had to ride all night to get there. Not for him either, as he has better things to do than perform autopsies. But he always was soft-hearted where the Black Aelf are concerned."

Sir Fits-William smirked. "It is laudable how you protect your friend. Do you think he will be as loyal to you?"

Robin leaned forward, and almost whispered his response. "There is no need for either of us to protect the other, because we did nothing wrong."

"We'll see about that."

Sir Fits-William strode out of the room, leaving Robin alone in the flickering torchlight, his face once again a mask of cold indifference.

Erich relaxed as the inquisitor walked in, his bottom sliding to the front edge of the chair. The large man loomed over him from behind, his voice sharp and commanding.

"I am Sir Fits-William. You've been traveling with Robin for days. Don't play the fool with me. What do you know of Lord Slovak's murder?"

Erich shook his head. "Lord Slovak? This is the first time I have heard of it. I don't know anything about it."

Sir Fits-William came around to face Erich, then suddenly slapped his hand on the table, nearly making Erich jump. "Don't lie to me. Robin is no ordinary thief. That one has the air of a killer. Tell me the truth and I will let you go. Who does he work for? Who hired him?"

Erich slowly raised his head. "Robin? He works for the Assassins' Guild in Voldair, of course. But he would only execute a sanctioned contract, and he has not been out of my company for any significant amount of time since he joined me here a week ago. I am sorry, there is just no way he could have gone on a killing spree."

Sir Fits-William leaned in. "Then how do you explain this?" He slammed the bloodied dagger onto the table.

Erich looked at the dagger with interest. "I've never seen that before. Robin certainly would never carry anything so ostentatious. I think you are looking for someone trying to make a name for themselves. Only they would think to use a weapon like that."

Sir Fits-William watched him closely. "So you've been holding hands for a week together, is that what I am to believe? You never separated, even for an hour?"

Erich thought about it. "There were several times we separated to gather ingredients, but he was not gone long enough to get the ingredients and kill someone. I think you are on the wrong path, Sir Fits-William.

"Think, Erich. We have witnesses who observed a hooded figure matching Robin's height and build. Three killings, all just happening to occur while Robin was in town. You're not stupid. What do your instincts say?"

Erich spoke softly, looking Sir Fits-William in the eyes. "My instincts say you are lazily going after the assassin you know is in town because he has not been circumspect about his movements or whereabouts, instead of doing the work searching for the assassin who is likely getting away while you dither here. If you would like, I can sell you a potion allowing you to better judge whether we are being truthful, but it would be a waste of ten turots."

Sir Fits-William scowled. It was clear he would not get any answers from these two. He walked out of the room, slamming the door behind him.

❧❧

Two days later, Erich and Robin were sharing a table at the Tortoise Palace, discussing their misadventures. Robin raised a glass. "A toast, to our continued friendship."

"To our friendship," Erich agreed.

Then Robin asked, "What did you end up reporting on that aelf woman? Did you turn everything over to Sir Fits-William?"

"No," Erich replied, his eyes growing dark. "The guards took much of my equipment, and damaged what they couldn't carry. It will take me months to replace some of those lenses. They were custom made by the dwarves at Snowy Pass. I sent an owl, but it is over two-weeks flight alone. I may have to travel there just to decrease the correspondence times."

Robin nodded. "I understand. So did you tell them it was blue-seed poison?"

Erich shook his head. "I told them that this unfortunately seems to be what it looks like. She was attacked and killed by wild dogs. I didn't want the Black Aelf to start looking for you."

Robin blinked. "What do you mean?"

Erich smiled. Come on my friend. You had a number of contracts to complete and showed up the day after I sent my request. You were already in Cairthorn preparing and tracking your victims. Not sure how you managed to pull the others off while you were with me, but it was easy enough to deduce.

The dagger was the final clue. Only the guild masters send those to be used. They wanted an example made. I wonder what he did."

Robin shook his head. "I was lucky. I went to the Plum House to get some plum brandy. As I was leaving, I noticed him going up to a room, so I turned around and followed him. He never even saw me. One minute he was lying down waiting for a princess, and the next, he was dead with the dagger through his heart."

"And the others?"

"Much easier. Had wine delivered to some merchants who have been selling fake artifacts. They were known for their love of exotic wines. Laced the wine with enough Butterlilly root to kill ten people. Fortunately, they were the only ones drinking that night."

"For swindling people? That seems a bit harsh."

"One of the people they swindled happened to be the wife of the commander of Stone Brook. He was none to happy and wanted them taken care of. Now they are."

"How about the aelf woman?"

"It was her husband actually. It seems he is not fond of humans. He rode down some women and children south of Gold Keep. Killing him might set off a larger conflict with the Black Aelf, so we went for the next best thing. It was important to make it clear it wasn't humans. I would have staged it with the grendlaar, but there aren't any near Cairthorn."

"I see," Erich said. "Well, I guess there is only one thing to do." Raising his glass again, he spoke brightly, "To our friendship."

The End

# ROBIN'S INITIATION
by
Roger Stockman

Robin sat in a cave with his horse to shelter them from the torrential downpour. He had tried riding through the rain, but it soon became nearly impossible to see which direction he was going. He needed to reach the merchant caravan before it arrived in the city of Stone Brook. It was already slow going through the mountains, and now the rain delayed him even longer. The Guild in Voldair would not look favorably upon him if he failed in his first mission. In this mission for the Guild, he was to locate the merchant in a caravan heading to Stone Brook. Once he found the merchant, he was to kill him. Robin didn't know the reason the Guild wanted him dead. It was not his place to question.

Robin had been training with the Guild for the last five years. He found a home with the Guild after he ran away from his master in the Black Woods at twelve. His life as an orphan hadn't been too bad, he supposed. However, by the time he turned twelve, he realized a life of indentured servitude was not for him. He had sneaked into a wagon of a merchant caravan departing the Black Woods. Robin managed to stay hidden until the caravan reached Voldair. When one of the wagon masters discovered him, he turned him over to the Guild. Training with the Guild had been arduous, but he had learned many useful skills he would never have learned as an indentured servant.

Robin sat at the mouth of the cave and watched the rain continue to pour. It still showed no signs of stopping, so he went to get some rest at the back of the cave. He lay on his bedroll, trying to catch a few minutes of sleep. The smell of the cave reminded him of the time the Guild had forced him to sleep in an alleyway for some minor infraction. It was the odor of urine and mold. Suddenly, he sensed some movement near the cave entrance. Robin got up. He was as still as a mouse and hid in the shadows at the rear of the cave. He kept his eyes focused toward the front to catch sight of a possible intruder. A shadowy figure crept inside, crouched in the dimness. The figure inched toward Robin's horse and began to open the saddlebags. Robin slipped his short sword from its scabbard and crouched low.

Brandishing his blade in front of him, Robin pounced toward the figure. The intruder only had a split second to turn around. Beneath the hood of the stranger's cloak, Robin saw the angular features of an aelf. Judging from the pungent, musky odor of the black nut, it must be a Black Aelf. Memories of his childhood in the Black Woods came flooding back into Robin's mind. He thought twice about killing this intruder. He had grown up with Black Aelf. Did he really have it in him to kill one? In Robin's moment of hesitation, the aelf quickly pulled a dagger from his belt and lunged toward Robin. Robin dodged to the right, but not quickly enough. The aelf's dagger sliced deep on the left side of Robin's leather armor along his rib cage. Fortunately, the armor prevented any injury. The aelf came for him again. Robin, more prepared this time, slammed his short sword into the aelf's hand which was holding the dagger. The aelf cried out in pain and jumped back toward Robin's horse.

Robin had the advantage now. As fast as lightning, Robin drew a dagger from his belt with his left hand, leapt toward the aelf, and feinted with his sword to the aelf's left. The aelf used his dagger to parry Robin's short sword. A split second after the aelf parried Robin's feint, Robin slammed the dagger in his left hand into the aelf's right eye socket. The aelf crumpled lifelessly to the ground. Robin felt no qualms about killing the aelf now. He was defending himself, after all.

Robin's heart now felt like the hooves of a galloping horse hammering on the hard ground. He grimaced. He really had to learn how to control his heartbeat. Robin knew he had to stay calm in all situations if he was to have a successful career with the Guild. Robin returned to his bedroll and sat on it cross-legged while taking deep breaths in order to bring his heartbeat down. Once his heart slowed, he lay down again to try to catch a few winks before setting off. Robin slept fitfully for a few hours when he sensed the rain beginning to slacken. He arose and approached the mouth of the cave. He peered into the darkness and saw it was still raining, but not enough to keep him from resuming his travels. Robin retrieved his bedroll and secured it to his horse. After mounting, he rode out into the blackness.

After an hour of traveling through the steady rain, Robin noticed the sun peeking above the eastern horizon. In the distance, he saw the mountainous terrain giving way to foothills. Soon he would be able to set his horse at a gallop to make up for lost time and, hopefully, reach the caravan before it reached the city.

After another hour of slow riding, Robin was approaching the foothills. He sensed a change in his environment. Robin focused on his surroundings as he rode. Then it came to him. There had been constant small wildlife around before, but he had noticed none recently. It may be nothing, but the Guild had taught him to trust his instincts. Maybe there were other humans in the area. This would be a good place for brigands to set up. As a lone rider, he would be easy pickings. Or so they would think. Robin continued to ride as if he suspected nothing, but he paid special attention to the surrounding terrain. He noticed a ridge behind him and to his left. It was about two hundred yards away, but that was still within distance of a good longbowman. Robin was just about to kick his horse into a gallop when he heard a faint whistling coming toward him. He tried to duck away from it, but he still felt something hard hit him, like a troll had punched him in the shoulder with its fist. The force of the impact flung Robin off his horse, and he landed hard on the rocky terrain. The collision with the ground knocked all the wind out of his lungs. Robin sensed his horse galloping away, and fast. Robin looked at his left shoulder and saw an arrow protruding from it. He had to think quickly, and he decided his best course of action would be to play dead. Robin was, however, able to draw his dagger surreptitiously from its sheath. He then waited for his attackers.

Soon, he heard voices approaching him. "You couldn't have killed him at that range, Flynt."

"Maybe he hit his head when he fell," said another voice.

"Flynt and Zeke, you go catch that horse. There may be something valuable in there," said the first voice. Robin heard the sounds of two horses galloping off in the same direction where his horse had run off. One of the useful skills the Guild had taught him was the ability to interpret sounds around him when he was unable to see. He listened more intently. He heard another horse approaching him. No, it was more than one. Two horses, Robin decided. He felt capable enough to deal with those odds, but the arrow embedded in his shoulder was a wild card he couldn't control.

"Go check him out," the first voice commanded.

"A-alright, b-boss," the other man stuttered.

Robin heard the man dismount and approach him. He sensed the man kneeling next to him and leaning into him. Robin plunged his dagger into the man's neck. The man squelched out a cry as he grabbed his neck with both hands in a futile attempt to stop the spurting blood. Robin looked quickly to the other man, who was still sitting atop his horse. "Jax!" He shouted as he tried to dismount quickly. The man got his left foot tangled in the stirrup and tumbled to the ground. Seeing his opening, Robin threw his dagger to the ground, drew his short sword with his right hand, and pounced toward the other man on the ground. The man was able to recover quickly and draw a long dagger, which he held out in front of him. Robin adroitly batted the dagger aside with his short sword. Robin was now atop the man, but he was too close to be able to use his short sword effectively. Robin dropped the short sword and drew another of his daggers from his belt. He thrust the dagger into the man's left eye.

Robin slowly stood up and retrieved his short sword from the ground. He saw the other two men riding back toward him. The arrow in Robin's back was draining the energy from him, and he realized he wouldn't be able to successfully fight off two men at once in his condition. Robin spun to the horse of the man he had just killed. Robin saw a long bow and a quiver of arrows fastened to the horse. It was fortunate for him the Guild training included the use of many types of weapons. He grabbed the long bow and an arrow from the quiver. The riders were close enough to do a killing shot, but Robin wondered if he would have the strength to draw the bow. It was do or die, he decided.

Robin grimaced as he drew the arrow back in the bow and aimed at one of the riders. Once he had the head of one of the riders in his sights, he let the arrow loose. Everything seemed to move in slow motion for Robin as he watched the arrow fly toward its target. It appeared to be going slightly off target, but then suddenly it hit the other man in the left shoulder, which un-horsed him. Robin knew he would not have enough strength to draw another arrow, but he decided to make a show of it anyway. He reached into his quiver and nocked the arrow. The last man apparently decided not to take his chances because he veered off and headed for the ridgeline.

Robin dropped the bow and arrow and fell to his knees, exhausted. After a few moments, he checked to ensure both men near him were actually dead. Then he rode one of the brigand's horses out to the man he had shot. He found the man on the ground, unconscious. Robin slit the man's throat with his dagger. He knew his first order of business was to treat the wound in his shoul-der. He broke off the back end of the arrow. Then he tore strips of cloth from the dead brigand's clothes and tied a makeshift bandage around the wound. Full treatment of his wound would have to wait until after he completed his mission and returned to Voldair. Robin's horse was nowhere to be seen, so he scavenged what he could from the remaining brigands' horses and rode off on one of them.

Robin traveled at a swift pace for the rest of the day. He hoped to find the merchant caravan soon. His new horse was beginning to show signs of fatigue. His pace was slowing, and the horse was sweating and foaming at the mouth. In any case, Robin would have to find another horse to return to Vol-dair. His current horse would be in no shape to make the return trip.

Off in the distance, Robin saw the city of Stone Brook looming large but saw no sign of the merchant caravan he was searching for. Nevertheless, he continued to ride hard toward the city despite his own fatigue creeping in. Within a half an hour, the sun was setting behind him, and he was entering the low hills around Stone Brook. Off in the distance to the northwest, Robin saw smoke rising from the hills. Perhaps the merchant caravan had camped for the night before entering the city. Robin decided it would be best to approach on foot. He took the light crossbow which was fastened to the brigand's horse. He also grabbed a handful of bolts. He loaded one of them into the crossbow and stuffed the rest into his backpack. He then dismounted and crept toward the smoke.

Robin was certain they would have sentries posted, so he would try to deal with them one at a time. He heard singing not too far ahead of him. Robin crouched down and used the terrain and dimness around him for cover. He crawled toward the singing. As he got nearer, he could make out the words of a drunken voice caterwauling. It was the song of the Knights of Wren and their victory over the Black Aelf at the bridge over the Blue Lake during the Great War. Robin found a location where he would be able to brace the crossbow and see the man howling away.

*With all our courage and our strength,*

*We must defend the lake of blue.*

*We will fight until our deaths.*

*The Black Aelf scourge will ne'er pass through!*


*Oh, we are the Wrens on a Bridge*

*And we are standing so steadfast.*

*We shan't give them even an inch.*

*The curséd aelf will soon be smashed!*

Just at this moment, Robin fired the bolt. It caught the sentry in in the neck. The man collapsed to the ground. Robin advanced on the man and slit his throat to ensure he was dead. He took the man's cloak and instantly caught the scent of black nut as he swirled it over his shoulders. That was interesting. Why would the sentry's cloak smell of black nut? He placed the hood over his head and found comfort in the aroma. He also found a bottle next to the dead sentry. Robin picked it up and sniffed it. The pungent odor of spice invaded his nostrils. Rum. Robin took a swig and showered some of it on his torso. Then he began stumbling toward the fire he could now see in the distance. Robin began singing the same song the sentry had been singing with the same raspy, drunken voice.

*The Black Aelf are a loathsome lot.*

*And they are hated through and through.*

*And in our snare they shall be caught.*

*And when they flee, we shall pursue!*

"Klaus, is that you? Are you drunk on guard duty again?" a voice called from the darkness. "The Master will have you drawn and quartered for sure this time. Especially if you're singing that song again!" Robin continued stumbling toward the voice until he came upon another sentry. He covertly drew a dagger from his belt. Robin staggered right up to the man. "Klaus, what are you doing?" Then Robin thrust his dagger behind the edge of the leather cuisse on the sentry's left thigh and severed his femoral artery. Simultaneously, Robin placed his left hand over the man's mouth to silence any cry. Robin slowly lowered the man to the ground and delivered the finishing blow.

Robin now saw a ring of wagons a short distance away. He ditched the cloak and walked through the shadows until he reached a wagon. One man was drowsily sitting at a fire in the center of the ring of wagons. Robin slowly and covertly moved around the outside of the ring of wagons. He had been told how to identify the merchant's wagon in the caravan. It would be the largest wagon with wooden sides, instead of canvas. It would also probably be the closest one to the city.

After only a few minutes, Robin found the wagon. At the rear of the wagon, one guard was safeguarding the door. He would have to dispatch the sentry quickly and quietly to gain entry inside to his target. Robin decided the best approach would be to try to lure the guard away from the door. Robin retreated behind a tree and reloaded the crossbow. He then picked up a stone from the ground and threw it off to his left. It made a loud *thwunk* sound as it hit a tree. The sound drew the attention of the sentry. He began moving off in the direction from which it came. Robin tracked the sentry with the crossbow, keeping him in its sights. When the guard was about fifty feet from the wagon, he let the bolt fly. The bolt caught the guard in the side of the neck. The guard tried to call out, but he was unable to make a sound because he was gargling on his own blood. Robin rushed to the guard quickly and delivered the coup de grâce.

Robin then made his way back to the wagon. He tried the door, but it was locked. Robin procured his lockpicking tools from his belt and unlocked the door, another useful skill he had learned from the Guild. He swung the door open to find a Black Aelf sitting in a chair. The aelf looked up, surprised. After a moment, the aelf stood and exclaimed, "Robin! Is that you? Where have you been, boy?" Robin looked at the Black Aelf incredulously. It was his old master. "Have you come to grovel for your position back?" he continued haughtily.

Overcoming his incredulity, Robin replied, "Master Dark Leaf, it is curious finding you here."

"You didn't come to find me?"

"No, I've come here to kill you."

"Kill me? Why? I never treated you with anything but kindness, boy."

"Stop calling me 'boy'!"

"But I treated you like a father would treat his own son."

"You were no father to me, Dark Leaf."

"Robin, my boy, come sit down here with me. We can discuss all of this now."

"Shut up! Let me think," Robin spat back. Dark Leaf approached Robin. "Stop!" Robin warned.

"Please come and sit."

Confused, Robin started walking toward Master Dark Leaf. He didn't know what to think. Why would the Assassin's Guild send him here to kill his old master? As Robin neared Dark Leaf, he noticed something glinting off the lantern light hidden in Dark Leaf's cloak. Suddenly, Dark Leaf swung his right arm quickly toward Robin. Robin narrowly avoided the dagger which was aimed at his throat by leaning back slightly.

"Did you really think you could actually kill me, boy?" Dark Leaf grabbed a short sword from the table and started swinging it at Robin. Robin swiftly drew his short sword with his right hand and a fencing dagger with his left. Dark Leaf thrust his short sword toward Robin. Robin tried to parry it with the dagger in his left hand, but the wound in his shoulder slowed him. He could only redirect it slightly so it caught him on his left side. He felt the blade cut into his ribcage. Robin cried out in pain. The blade must be enchanted to cut through his armor. Either that or Dark Leaf had managed to hit the same spot in which the aelf thief had managed to cut him two nights earlier. Robin knew he would have to kill Dark Leaf quickly because the other guards would be on him soon. Robin caught a break because Dark Leaf had difficulty dislodging the blade from Robin's armor. Robin braced himself against the wall of the wagon and kicked Dark Leaf back with his right foot. He then swung his own short sword hard at Dark Leaf's throat. The sword caught Dark Leaf on the side of his neck, and blood began spurting from the wound. Robin pulled Dark Leaf's sword from his side and threw it onto the floor.

Dark Leaf fell to the floor of the wagon. Robin was on him in an instant and, with his fencing dagger, pierced Dark Leaf between the fourth and fifth rib in his chest and thrust upward. Dark Leaf crumpled lifelessly. The Guild would need proof he had successfully completed his mission. Robin tried to remove Dark Leaf's signet ring, but his ring finger was too bloated. Instead, Robin used his dagger to sever the finger from the hand and tucked it into a pouch on his belt. He heard the guards mustering outside. Robin bolted from the wagon and stumbled to the front of it. He tried to mount one of the horses fastened to the front of the wagon but realized he was unable to because of his fatigue from the all-night travel and his compounding wounds. Robin climbed up on the wagon tongue. He shimmied himself along the wagon tongue until he managed to reach one of the horses. With a bit of effort, he was able to mount one of the horses from there. He cut the horse loose from the yoke and rode off. He left the sounds of the shouting guards behind him. As he rode off into the darkness, he had many questions swirling around in his head. *Why had the Guild sent him, of all people, to kill Dark Leaf? Why did they want Dark Leaf dead? Why did they not tell him who his target was?* The answers would have to wait until he returned to Voldair. That is if the Assassin's Guild would deign to answer them, but he assumed they would not. Robin continued to ride off into the night with his many thoughts dancing in his mind.

∾

Robin awoke in bed. He squinted his eyes a few times to bring his eyes into focus. He was in a small room. To his right was a table with a small basin. Sitting in a chair on the other side of the room was a woman dressed in a simple, drab dress.

"Ah, good. You've awoken," she said.

"Where am I?" Robin asked.

"You're back in Voldair. The Guild Council will be wanting to talk to you soon."

"How—how long have I been back?"

"Three days. You've been asleep the whole time. We've managed to remove the arrow shaft from your shoulder and treat the wound in your side, but you'll likely be in bed for several more days."

"No—" Robin attempted to get out of bed, but his world began swirling about him.

The woman came toward Robin. "I *said* you'll likely be in bed for several more days." She lowered Robin back into the bed. "You should make a full recovery, but you'll need time. Now just get some sleep."

࿇

The next time Robin awoke, he opened his eyes to see the Master of Novices staring down on him. "It's about time, boy. The Guild Council will see you now. Get dressed, and I'll meet you outside your door." The man turned and left the room.

Robin took his time getting out of the bed and getting dressed. He still felt a little woozy, but he managed to stay on his feet. He exited the room and found the Master of Novices waiting for him just outside the door. "Follow me, Robin. The Guild Council will be expecting a full accounting of the mission."

"I understand, Master Joppa."

"Make sure you leave nothing out. They'll be able to tell if you're withholding anything, and I don't need to tell you the consequences of that."

Robin nodded his understanding. Then Master Joppa led Robin through the halls until they came to a double door with a guard on each side. The guards made no move to stop them. Master Joppa placed his hands on both doors and pushed them open. Robin and Master Joppa stepped inside the large room. Robin recognized the room as the one where the Guild Council assigned him his first mission. At the far side of the room, opposite the double doors, there was a long table. Behind the table sat twelve members of the Guild Council. The empty thirteenth chair belonged to Master Joppa, who stood beside Robin now. Master Joppa left Robin's side and took his place at the table.

Master Joppa then addressed the council. "The novice Robin has returned from his first mission. He is here to give a full accounting."

"Proceed," one of the other council members commanded. Robin began to give a full accounting of everything which transpired during the mission. As Master Joppa advised, Robin didn't leave anything out. However, the memory of the three to four-day time period between his retreat from the merchant camp and when he first awoke in Voldair was pretty much a blur. Fortunately, the council didn't seem too perturbed by that.

"To the best of your knowledge, this is a full accounting of everything which happened during your mission?" Master Joppa asked.

"Yes, Master."

Another council member, Robin thought his name was Master Ranulph, spoke up. "Very well. It appears you were partially successful in your mission."

"Partially—" Robin started but was immediately cut off after a stern look from Master Joppa.

Master Ranulph continued, "You returned with Dark Leaf's signet ring, which shows success. Our spies have also been able to determine that Dark Leaf is, indeed, dead. However, you made quite a mess of things along the way. You returned with an arrow in your shoulder and a wound in your side. Once arriving back in Voldair, it took you three days to recover from your injuries. You also left a trail of bodies along the way. This has drawn unwelcome attention to the Voldair Assassin's Guild."

Robin bit back a retort. He knew failing in your first mission resulted in "dismissal" from the guild. So he held his tongue and hoped for the best.

"Therefore, it is the judgment of this council that you are to continue as a novice under the tutelage of the Master of Novices until such a time you are ready for a second mission. You should know, anything other than full success in your second mission will result in dismissal from the guild. That is all. You will report to Master Joppa in the morning to continue your training."

Robin gulped. It appeared he had narrowly avoided death. He had been looking forward to becoming a full member of the Assassin's Guild, but now he had to continue his training for who knew how long. No, this wasn't what Robin had envisioned at all, but what could he do about it?

"I understand. Thank you, Master," Robin replied. He then turned around and exited the chamber.

The End

# SIVLE AND ALLIANDRE
by
Daniel E. Myers

"I don't think. We are going to make. As much as you. Thought we were." Alliandre said in between blows to his shield.

The Tullamore's snake like head struck Alliandre's shield again, its long neck, longer than Alliandre was tall, twisting to try and get around the slightly curved wood and steel plank. The metal and wood smoking wherever the acidic saliva of the beast dripped. Alliandre deftly kept the shield face perpendicular to the beast's gaping maw. Repeatedly, he struck the beast with his sword, but the blows bounced off the tough scales of the demi-dragon. Sivle's spells, other than a small amount of damage from his spirit missiles, were likewise having no effect.

The two friends continued fighting the Tullamore, formed from the mating of two different dragons. This one from a highland dragon and a wood dragon, the dwarves had said. It was gray, like most Tullamores, with a body nearly four paces long and two wide. They had come prepared to fight it, bringing flasks of oil with fuses. Sivle had even purchased a scroll with a fire blast. Neither was effective. Sivle suspected the parentage was incorrect. The grey eyes, for one thing, bespoke of a stone dragon, which would explain its resistance to his flame spells. The large pair of horns on its snout bespoke of a swamp dragon, which would explain the acidic spittle. But where it got its nearly impenetrable hide from, Sivle had no idea.

The Tullamore reared back on its hind legs and lashed its neck out again. It finally managed to get past Alliandre's shield craft. It caught the top corner of the shield in its mouth, which was nearly as large as the shield. The great lizard tossed Alliandre around, trying to shake him off the shield. Alliandre could smell the acrid breath of the creature as it tried to dislodge the shield from his arm. He knew if he lost the shield, the beast's massive jaws would make short work of his armor, and him. He held on desperately while throwing hammer blow after hammer blow against the long neck of the monster. None of them had any effect. Finally, the shield gave way and a large section splintered beneath the steel rim.

Alliandre changed tactics and launched into a sparrow dive, driving the sword point into the chest of the creature. The tip managed to push two scales aside, and a spot of red colored the Tullamore's previously unblemished hide. Enraged with pain, the beast lunged again at Alliandre, getting past the damaged shield, catching a pauldron in its teeth. Alliandre groaned as the metal yielded to the mouthful of teeth. Blood flowed from his shoulder as the pauldron tore loose. The beast's teeth raked his skin, acidic spittle burning in the wound. Alliandre winced at the teeth ripping, rather than cutting, furrows in his shoulder.

Seeing the pointlessness of continuing, Sivle pulled Alliandre away from the monster's side. He cast a spirit shield to protect them as they made their retreat. Tullamores varied in strengths and weaknesses according to their parentage. Some could even breath fire or poison gas like a proper dragon. Fortunately, this Tullamore had not displayed and breath ability yet. But Sivle was taking no chances as the tullamore turned to follow them.

"We can still beat it," Alliandre shouted in frustration. His last thrust had partially dislodged a scale, and his blade had sunk nearly an inch into the beast.

"We can beat it after we have reprovisioned." Sivle struggled to pull the much larger fighter away. "Let's heal up. I am sure he will still be here tomorrow. You will not wed Marion if you end up in the beast's stomach."

Grudgingly, Alliandre turned and the two retreated out of the cave and back into the open air, the beast in pursuit. Fastening the spirit shield to the cave opening to prevent the beast from following them, the two ran to their horses. They had not tied the horses, and they were happy to see the two animals had not been frightened away by the shrieks within the Tullamore's cave.

Assessing the damage to his friends' shoulder, Sivle scowled as he noticed the skin bubbling from the acidic burns. Over a foot shorter than Alliandre, Sivle had to raise his head to see the wounds. Sivle's hand glowing with fauna spirit and aether, he touched it to Alliandre's wound. The gashes slowly closed and the skin mostly returned to Alliandre's natural olive color. It would be hours before the healing completed, but the wounds were closed and the burns reduced.

It fatigued Sivle, using his own fauna spirit in this way, but he would recover. Unlike mage spells, which he had to memorize, he prayed for his priest spells each day, allowing him to cast them at will. Their only limit was the experience of the priest. Spells requiring Fauna Spirit however, required the caster to draw upon much more of his own life force.

Alliandre struggled to pull himself up, as his injured shield arm was the same one he used to grab the pommel to swing his leg over the high-backed, military-style saddle. As if sensing his injury, his spottled Percheron stood still until Alliandre was situated in the saddle.

Sivle mounted his brown Arabian, just a riding horse really, but trained for war, nonetheless. Together the two friends galloped away as quickly as the mountainous terrain would allow. It was already late in the day, and the spirit shield would not hold long. They hoped the flightless Tullamore would decide to lick its wounds as well. They slowed down while descending the sloped hills to the valley below. There they would be able to increase the speed for a while. If they rode straight through, they could get to the fort at Snowy Pass by midnight.

"Are we going to end up with any money left?" Alliandre asked. Over six and a half feet tall, and heavily muscled, he had dedicated the last ten of his eighteen years to becoming a knight. He had left the Freehold of Dragonsbane nine months ago, rejected by their leaders despite bearing the Del Nileppez name. Now, he hoped to complete a quest to gain his knighthood. Immediately, he sought out Sivle, who had been High Priest of the Foresight Temple until just a month ago. The promise of a score of turots each for slaying the Tullamore brought them here.

Sivle caught the attention of a famous mage, Toron, who agreed to train him for a small fee. Alliandre spent weeks trying to locate the tullamore's lair while Sivle trained. He found the lair four days ago. Then they began their preparation. They spent half of Sivle's share on the worthless scroll, and now had to spend more on another. Perhaps lightning this time. Then there was the matter of Alliandre's damaged armor.

"We will have plenty, though not as much as we had hoped." Sivle assured him. Standing just three inches over five feet tall, his slightly pointed ears exposed his half aelf heritage. It was his heritage which made him look years younger than Alliandre, despite being three years his senior. "We will reprovision tomorrow and come back in two days."

"Let's make it three days," Alliandre stated. "I want to camp at the base of the mountain." Alliandre pointed down to a small outcropping. "Then we can ride up in the morning. Maybe we can catch it sleeping."

Sivle nodded. He didn't see the wisdom in it but had learned to trust Alliandre's judgement in martial matters. There was no question Sivle was the more intellectual of the two, but in matters of tactics and strategy, years of study made up Alliandre's inequality in gray matter. They rode through the rest of the day in silence, with Alliandre circling back several times to ensure the creature was not stalking them.

જ૦જ

They rested the next day, with Alliandre nursing his shoulder and Sivle using the last of his turots on a lightning scroll. Rummaging through their packs, Alliandre found another Pauldron, but it was of a different style. Not having the money to buy a new one, they brought it to an armorer to have it adjusted to fit the rest of Alliandre's suit of plate mail. Knowing Alliandre was trying to rid the threat of the Tullamore, the armorer only charged him a handful of dolcots. He even provided an old steel shield.

The white dwarves who lived around Snowy Pass were happy to see the two friends return and asked to be regaled by their story of fighting the beast. Alliandre was careful not to say too much. They didn't want the other adventurers there getting any ideas. Only one other group looked ready to go, but the two fighters were in mis-matched armor and their priest was clearly newly raised. Alliandre warned them of the creature's tough scaled hide.

The first fighter, Dorra he said his name was, held out his sword. "Fire Storm has already killed a dozen beasts. I'm sure this one will be no different."

Alliandre smiled. "Trust not in the flame. It is somewhat resistant."

"Then I will rely on Geraldine. Between the two of us, we will find its weakness and exploit it." The other fighter, a stocky red head with bright blue eyes, smiled shyly. Her perfectly aligned teeth, brilliantly white, bespoke of a wealthy family. Alliandre wondered why she had chosen this profession, particularly being so young.

Neither of them looked even as old as Alliandre. He had trained with the sword since he was seven and had spent five years at Dragonsbane as a squire. They did not feel Alliandre was worthy of knighthood though, despite the fact he was training the other squires and even several knights. He doubted either of these two had his skill or experience.

He tried to warn them again. "Don't be too hasty. Why don't you wait for Sivle and me, then we can go together and overwhelm the beast. The reward is certainly enough to cover all of us."

Dorra answered him emphatically. "We don't need any help. You were not able to defeat the creature, which is why you want our help. We can do it without you."

Alliandre reached out his arm to clasp wrists with the two. "Then may you fare better than my friend and I did yesterday."

⁊⸱⸰

The next day, they headed out after first meal. Stopping by the armorer, Alliandre tried on his repaired armor, discovering it fit perfectly. After paying the dwarf, he joined Sivle outside, and they rode leisurely to the outcropping Alliandre had pointed to the night before. They set up camp inside the natural barrier provided by the rocks, moving a few large stones to improve the defensive wall. Sivle took first watch while Alliandre prepared a meal of bread, cured meats and cheese, and a wineskin full of a strong, sweet mead.

After the dinner was eaten and the camp secured, Alliandre took out a small chest and opened it. Inside, wrapped carefully in linens, was a small painting of his love, Marion the Virtuous.

"Fret not, my friend." Sivle told him. "When we finish with this tullamore, we can speak to the Dwarven king. He may have a quest, and a knighting by the dwarves is just as good as any of the orders."

"Perhaps, but what if he has no quest?" Alliandre again looked at Marion. It was for her he risked life and limb to gain knighthood. He had promised her he would become a knight and wed her as soon as she was of age. But Dragonsbane had rejected him, and there were few orders who would take in a rejected squire. He still had time, as she was only thirteen, and still two years away from when she would be eligible for courting. Two years was plenty of time to find a quest and complete it. Kissing the image, he wiped it off and carefully wrapped it before putting it back into the chest. "So far, the only quest we have heard of is from the barbarian king to the west."

"It has only been a month, my friend. We will find you a quest. For now, let's get to sleep"

The night passed uneventfully, other than a small snow owl which had decided to perch above their makeshift camp. It flew off several times, returning each time with a small rodent, which it noisily ate before flying off again. Alliandre wasn't concerned about the owl, but the smell of the dead animals could bring larger predators. Land Sharks were not common in the mountains, but there were other dire beasts which roamed the mountains this far north. Not the least of which were snow wolves. Alliandre could defeat one or two of them, but they traveled in packs of ten to twenty.

As the sun cast its light across the valley, Alliandre roused Sivle. The former High Priest began his prayers while Alliandre set out more food and tended to their horses. Sivle completed his prayers for the spells he would need and the two discussed the day. His mage spells he had memorized the day before. They remained in his memory, but his priest spells he was required to pray for each day.

"What is the plan today?" Sivle asked.

Alliandre shrugged. "We will see if the Tullamore is harmed by the lightning. If it is, that will take care of it, and we will be done."

Sivle smiled. "Not much of a plan, my friend."

"It had a tough time getting around my shield. While its mouth is large, it doesn't open wide enough to catch my whole shield, so as long as I can keep the shield facing it, I should be fine. Now we know slashing it does no good, I will focus on stabbing strikes. I think I can get through if I can dislodge a scale or two." Alliandre made a stabbing motion to reinforce his statement. "Once I can get a blade in, I can kill it."

Sivle nodded. It wasn't a great plan, but under the circumstances, it made sense. There just wasn't much to think about when facing any dangerous creature in its lair. Enter its lair, find the beast, and kill it. You could try to lure it outside, but they had tried baiting the beast the day before and only ended up wasting a perfectly good goat. Finishing his food, Sivle rose and went over to his horse. He mounted up and waited for Alliandre to follow.

"Coming, my friend?" Sivle asked.

"Yes. But I wanted to say thank you first. You left your station in Foresight as soon as I asked. I don't know why, but you have always helped me. I wanted to tell you I appreciate it."

"You were always there for me when I was younger. You did my chores when I was staying up late studying. You protected me from the squires and knights when they taunted me. And you have never treated me any different, despite my heritage. You have been my brother for as long as I can remember."

"But we are not brothers. We aren't even cousins."

We are both orphans, raised by Queen Arielle. That would be enough for me. But you are also the kindest, brave, and most honorable man I know. So you are my brother.

Smiling, Alliandre clasped wrists with his friend. "Orphan brothers then."

"Orphan brothers it is. And as long as I live, I will do whatever I can to help you get knighted. And I better be First Lord at your wedding."

"I promise." Releasing his friend's wrist, Alliandre spoke again. "I was just thinking. Do you have any cold spells?"

Sivle shook his head. "Just one used for killing small vermin, and some cantrips. I don't think it will do any good against a Tullamore. Particularly one used to the cold this far north."

Alliandre smiled and stood up. "I remembered swamp dragons are susceptible to cold. Maybe this one is too." Mounting his own horse, Alliandre continued. "I really wish we knew what dragons made this thing."

"Wishes in one hand and vreen dung in the other, Alliandre." Sivle smiled. "Which hand fills up first?"

Alliandre grinned at the old saying, and the two began their ride up the mountain. Having the advantage of knowing where the Tullamore cave was, they set their horses back fifty paces to avoid alerting the monster. Then they crept to the cave, moving as silently as armored men carrying metal weapons and shields could move. Reaching the mouth of the cave, Alliandre raised a gauntleted fist.

Signaling Sivle to stay where he was, the young fighter moved into the cave. Ten paces in, he lowered his arm again to let Sivle know how far behind to follow. The wide mouth of the cave let in the morning sun, but the light diminished as they move further in. Deeper than they had been before, they found the beast sleeping. On the ground nearby were the partially eaten bodies of the adventurers they had met two days earlier. Alliandre noticed Geraldine's face contorted in pain from her death. Her once white teeth now bloodstained, her smooth, fair skin grimy and sagging.

While Sivle said a prayer of the bodies, commending their spirits to the aether, Alliandre moved forward. Leaping, he thrust his sword into the sleeping beast. The blade nicked a scale and got between it and the underlying scale before sliding off. Alliandre recovered his footing and prepared to strike again as the enraged Tullamore, now fully awake, rose to all four legs, preparing to lash out its huge head at Alliandre.

The head snapped up and forward, as Alliandre had expected. He sidestepped the head and stepped up to thrust his sword again, this time into the rust colored area indicating where he had weakened the scale hide days before. Sparrow dive followed by fencer's thrust followed by steel rain. Over and over, his sword tip chipped away at the scales and moved them aside as they became partially dislodged. Then, the creature turned.

Alliandre barely managed to interpose his shield between the twin spikes on the tail snapping toward him. If not for the steel facing, the shield would have shattered. Instead, Alliandre cried in pain as the large spike penetrated the shield as well as his forearm, the round horn separating and shattering the bones at it penetrated, tearing the flesh rather than slicing it. Alliandre winced from the pain exploding from the bone as well as the muscle and tearing tendons and ligaments. The beast tried to pull its tail free, but it was caught in the shield and Alliandre's arm. Alliandre braced to avoid being dragged behind the creature, screaming in pain as the beast struggled.

The tail was five paces long and as thick as Alliandre at its base. Despite Alliandre's inhuman strength, the creature turned again, pulling Alliandre back towards its hind legs. Falling as his body was turned and pulled, Alliandre swung for the tail. Surprisingly, the blade found purchase and sliced a good way in. The Tullamore cried in pain, and finally dislodged the spike by slapping its tail up and down. Then, it stomped Alliandre with one of its hind legs, Alliandre barely interposed his shield in time. He watched helplessly while the spiked tail rose again. His shield trapped between his body and the Tullamore's foot; he would be unable to use it. He raised his sword instead, but his vision blurred.

Lightning filled the narrow cavern, slicing through the creature and exiting its tail. The beast recoiled, giving Alliandre the chance to free himself and roll to his feet. Alliandre moved to the head of the beast again. The area where he had thrust before was now a small wound, with electric burns at its perimeter. A leaping frog tongue drove Alliandre's sword three quarters of the way into the beast's chest.

The tullamore turned and writhed to dislodge the sword. It would not budge, but Alliandre lost his grip on it. Finally, the Tullamore rolled over, and disaster struck. Alliandre's sword, enchanted to resist damage and remain sharp, broke. The now useless handle rolled away awkwardly from the beast, the remaining blade shard changing its direction as it rolled. The Tullamore rose, eyes red with hate and pain, then snapped his head forward. Alliandre moved, interposing his shield, but the injured arm was too slow, and he found his entire torso in the jaws of the beast. Despite his armor, he could feel ribs breaking and flesh yielding to the dagger-like teeth.

The creature's jaws closing down on him, the image of his love, Marion, flashed in his mind. He pictured her worried face as they left for the White Hills. She was a princess, and he could not court her until he was ennobled somehow. It was all that drove him the last six years since they fled Vista. He hoped to find glory in battle to prove his worth, but now it was over. He imagined her face when she found out he was gone. He spoke a quiet apology to Marion as he coughed up blood and his eyes went black.

His eyes popped open again as a jolt went through him. Sivle had stepped forward and sent a charge of electricity through the blade shard which was still protruding from the monster. The tullamore roared as it reeled back in pain. Alliandre was forgotten as this new foe stepped forward. Crumpled on the ground, Alliandre could only watch as his priest friend, just learning to be a mage, faced off against the creature. Blood, mixed with the acidic saliva of the beast, created a metallic stench in the air.

Sivle struck first, using his spirit missile. The two points of light raced out and struck the Tullamore. The Tullamore's head sped forward and consumed Sivle's small round shield. Sivle released it from his arm, and for a moment, the Tullamore's mouth was blocked from closing. Using the opportunity, Sivle cast a small spell, sending a small blast of freezing aether toward the sword shard. It missed the shard, but the effect on the monster was unmistakable. A portion of the creature just froze.

Sivle cast another spell and touched the beast, this time on the neck. Once again, the beast recoiled as a section of its body turned solid. Twice more, Sivle touched the Tullamore, targeting the head of the beast, which had managed to dislodge the shield. One more touch and one side of the Tullamore's head was frozen, the beast falling. Dead. Alliandre had been right about the cold. Realizing his friend had not risen, Sivle rushed to Alliandre's side.

Sivle was not a powerful mage yet, but he had risen to the rank of High Priest in the temple at Foresight. His priestly skills were equal of any other High Priest, although he had favored long ignored war-priest spells. Still, he had not neglected the healing spells. Drawing on his own spirit, feeling the drain on his very life force, he pulled fauna spirit from the aether and lay his glowing hands on Alliandre. Soon, his friend was sitting up. Removing the now worthless armor, Sivle inspected the wounds on the torso further. Acid had dripped into them.

"I don't think we got paid enough to repair my armor." Alliandre stated, with only a touch of remorse. "And that was my last enchanted sword."

"We are alive, which means we have time to replace everything." Sivle reassured him. "Nothing says we have to go out and fight another monster tomorrow. Besides, I see Fire Storm."

Sivle poked around the cave as Alliandre recovered. Sure enough, he pulled a sword out of a pile of chewed up armor and weapons. Rummaging through the pile further, he found an axe and a large metal shield. Finally, just when he was going to quit, another sword handle caught his eye. Reaching down and pulling it up, he couldn't help but recognize the swirled pattern which had made the Steinvirki weapon smiths famous. "Here you go. Another sword for the collection."

Alliandre perked up. Walking gingerly over, he grabbed the sword from Sivle. "Silver Cross runes here," he said as he pointed to the markings on the blade. "We might not get to keep this one."

"Well then, at least we will get a sizeable ransom when we bring it back." Sivle smiled at his friend. If the sword had runes, it was enchanted. And the Silver Cross paladins were among the wealthier orders. Examining the runes, he saw the standard ones to harden and toughen a sword to resist breaking and chipping. But there were others, indicating fire and lightning. Eight runes in total ran down both sides of the blade. This was a powerful sword, and the paladins would be eager to get it back.

They searched the rest of the cave together. Among the bones, they found a ring lying on the ground. Finding nothing else of value, they got the horses and their ropes. Building a stretcher out of the small pine trees prevalent this far north, they loaded the Tullamore on the back. After building another stretcher for the three bodies of the previous party, they began the trek back to Snowy Pass.

Both Sivle and Alliandre were tired by the time they had reached the safety of the fort, Alliandre left Sivle to deal with the treasure. He went straight to the inn to rest and let the healing spells complete their work. Sivle returned to his teacher to see what enchantments might be on the weapons.

"Lord Sivle, why do you try my patience with these requests? Is it not enough I enlighten your mind to the wonders of the Forest Spirits?" His teacher looked across the table stacked with the ancient tomes he had been studying.

"Your forbearance please, Master Tolon," Sivle pleaded. "It is of immense value to me to see all of the skills you possess. Isn't this what the manuals teach us? We study the masters to learn what is possible."

Tolon smiled. "Lord Sivle, in order to truly understand the Forest Spirits, you must build upon what you already know. You cannot construct the parapets before the tower walls. Research the runes and you will gain more than the knowledge of the enchantments."

So Sivle went to the temple to research the runes. Hours later he emerged, excitement clear on his face. He nearly ran to the inn, to show his friend. He found Alliandre awake and gingerly putting new bandages on his still oozing wounds.

"Good news my friend," he proclaimed, "we have three enchanted weapons."

Then, picking up the sword, he pointed to the runes as he described what they did. "The sword is a powerful weapon, able to send out sheets of fire and lightning." Turning it over, he pointed out two more runes. "It is also a holy sword, focused on damaging creatures of aether. Three of these runes just harden the blade, but it is as hard as danium now. The last one keeps the blade sharp."

Then he put the sword down and picked up the axe. "The axe is enchanted to not only remain sharp and unbreaking but is also effective against stone creatures." Once again, Sivle pointed at each of the four runes in order as he explained what they did. "Firestorm is a flaming sword, not terribly powerful, but will burn with a flame. It is also hardened. The shield has just been spelled to resist damage, but it is a strong enchantment, see the two runes here intertwined?"

He almost felt bad about keeping Fire Storm, but the laws on treasure were clear. He regretted now they had not teamed up with the young adventurers. One last stop to the armorer. He thought he might trade the axe, and he had a hint of an idea to replace Alliandre's armor. He started over, but it was not to be.

The entire population of the fort, nearly sixty dwarves and a handful of visiting humans and aelf had shown up to greet them. Someone had laid the Tullamore on the street, and dwarven children were having fun bashing it with wooden hammers and axes. Thirty dwarven women swarmed Sivle, their natural animosity towards aelf, even half-aelf, forgotten for the moment. By the time they finished congratulating him, the armorer had joined the festivities.

Sivle did eventually convince him to make a trade for the enchanted axe. Two months later, after Sivle had completed his training, the friends rode down Snowy Pass to Brackenwater. They wore matching scale armor. It was gray and plain, but nearly impenetrable. Alliandre, for his part, also had a new flaming sword, and a large steel shield. He was better equipped to finish a quest, if they could find one, and had a pocket full of turots to boot.

"We turned a nice profit after all." Alliandre mused. "But I am still no closer to becoming a knight."

"Quit whining." Sivle smiled as he rebuked his friend. "We will go to Silver Cross Keep and return the sword, and maybe they will knight you. If not, I hear the Vreen are raising war parties in the south. Nothing like a good war to get one knighted."

"Well then, my orphan brother, let's go!"

The End

# GRENDALL AND VORINELLE
by
Daniel E. Myers

25th of Frendalo, Year 1124 After the Great War (AGW)

Just outside the Darklands

Grendall and Vorinelle crept slowly into the darkness. The two Copper Aelf wore their standard traveling clothes, which were deceiving. Vorinelle had spent the last several years apprenticing to the Thieves Guild in Cairthorn. His traveling clothes included a heavy leather gambeson with decorative silver polygons. The polygon placement was such that the coat acted as quite functional armor, particularly with the enchantments on the ornaments. Grendall had just become a full mage. She cast her best spell, spirit armor, when they entered. It usually shimmered, but as soon as they had entered the Darklands, the shimmer ceased. She hoped the protections did not fade as well.

The light from the enchanted stone they had thrown was barely visible, less than five paces away. The distance they could see it from had slowly shrunk as they got further into the Darklands. It seemed to be a steady five paces now, a tiny star in an immense black sky. They cautiously walked towards it. Upon reaching it, they checked their compass, marked their map, and tossed it again. By their estimation they were a hursmarc inside the Darklands.

As they crept up to the stone, they listened closely for signs of any activity. The Golden Aelf had taken over this land. To date, none who had stayed in the Darklands for more than a couple of hours had come out to tell the tale. They had been inside for several hours now. Grendall picked up the stone with a velvet gloved hand and once again tossed it ahead.

Clunk.

Vorinelle let out a small gasp. Clearly, the stone had hit something. As they approached, they could see a vague black shape in the faint light cast by the stone. Preparing for an attack, they separated, Vorinelle drawing his sword while Grendall pulled a glowing dagger from its sheath. Noting no movement, they deliberately approached. There appeared to be a black void next to the stone. Lifting the stone from the ground, they investigated it more closely. There was a cylindrical object which seemed to emanate darkness. Vorinelle placed his hand on the object, noting it was solid, feeling strangely warm.

Grendall pulled out a small wooden rod from its case and moved the tip towards the cylinder.

"Wait!" cautioned Vorinelle. "We can only use the wand once. Do we want to waste it on this?"

"Of course. Then we are returning to the keep. If the paladins want us to investigate further, we will, but only after they give us another of these."

"We are barely even inside the borders."

"Vorinelle, we have been inside the Darklands longer than anyone who has returned. Maybe that is why they don't return. They keep going until they run into something. We will return if the paladins wish us to, but we are going back to report what we have found."

Grendall placed the rod against the cylinder and yelped when the cylinder disappeared, revealing a naked aelf male lunging at Vorinelle. Vorinelle slashed wildly at the  emaciated body. Something blocked his sword, it bounced off with another clunk. Meanwhile, the aelf slumped forward before oozing to the ground. Grendall's heart was pounding madly. It was several seconds before she could speak.

"He looks dead."

"No, I can see him still breathing. He looks like a Great Aelf. What in the Spirits' name is a Great Aelf doing here?"

"I don't know. Should we try to help him or report it back to the paladins?"

"Let's try to help. He doesn't look too heavy. We could probably carry him back with us."

They moved closer to the body and found an invisible force around him.

"He's in a spirit cage I think." Grendall said after inspecting it more closely. "Chwala la hudd"

With a slight gush of wind, the aelf fell all the way to the ground with a groan.

"Tá sé go maith. We have you." Vorinelle whispered as he cradled the aelf's head.

Slowly rolling him on to his back then raising his shoulders, he got him into a sitting position. Grendall grabbed the aelf's arms and helped Vorinelle raise him to his feet so Vorinelle could hoist him over his shoulder. Carrying him, they followed their compass back towards the edge of the darkness. Almost an hour later, they emerged, seeing their horses in the outcropping of rock a hundred paces away.

"That's strange," mentioned Vorinelle, as he looked at the horses nearly fifty paces away. "I thought we had left the horses closer."

They carried the aelf to their horses, securing him in the saddle in front of Vorinelle. They estimated two days' travel back to Silver Cross Keep unencumbered, three with the aelf male in tow. They decided they would go to Westmoor first, hopefully running into a patrol of some sort. Riding the rest of the day and into the night, they stopped at the hamlet of Castaway.

There were no inns, so they set up their tent next to a cottage which had no smoke coming from the chimney. With the moon peeking above the horizon, Vorinelle agreed to take watch while Grendall slept the four hours until near dawn. They would strike camp and leave the hamlet before sunrise.

26th of Frendalo, Year 1124 AGW

Hamlet of Castaway

The night passed without incident for Grendall and Vorinelle; the sun rising in a clear blue sky. Seeing the stars in the west were not visible, Grendall whispered to herself, "Starlight in the west, day will be the best."

Vorinelle finished the old saying, "No stars in the morn, there's going to be a storm."

They smiled at each other. Since they met a month ago, they found they had a lot in common. Both had studied silver smithing under Bwento Sumiglene once they had completed deasghnáth pasáiste. Unaware of each other, they left the Copper Leaf Woods after they had completed Chegando a idade, traveling separately to the northeast, eventually reaching Cairthorn for their respective training. Excelling at their craft, both left Cairthorn when they heard the Paladins of the Silver Cross were hiring adventurers. They arrived at the keep on the same day, striking up a friendship waiting for an audience. Once they heard the task, they immediately joined up to investigate together.

Still smiling, they packed up everything, checking on their unconscious companion as they prepared to leave. Their ride into the night meant they could reach the town of Westmoor by evening. Even if they alternated carrying the unresponsive aelf on their horses, they could only walk. If they were lucky, they would run into a patrol on the road, otherwise, they would have to travel through the night if they wanted to reach the keep in even two days. Since they could do nothing about it, they went east towards Westmoor.

"Keep an eye out behind us." cautioned Vorinelle as they left on their journey. "The knights will not be happy if we made it four hours into the Darklands, only to let the Golden Aelf kill us while traveling back."

The sun was setting on the prairie behind them. As they had predicted, a storm hit them a few hours out of camp, slowing their pace even further. They tied the aelf over the saddle, Vorinelle walking while Grendall rode as they traversed up the first large hill. They travelled all day in the rain. It was getting on towards their evening meal, yet Westmoor was not even on the horizon. Then the rain ended. The sky to the west was clear, the east still dark and foreboding.

The land changed to intermittent hills and great valleys as they neared the Great Chasm. After reaching the top of the first major hill, Vorinelle got back into the saddle as they worked their way down to the wide valley, where he dismounted again. Tall moor grass covered the ground, which in the valleys was a bog. Their horses would sink to their knees, despite Vorinelle plunging a staff into the ground every five paces. Then they had to back the horses out to find more firm footing.

Twice during the day, the Great Aelf made some sort of vocalization. Neither of them could understand it. Both times he fell back into unconsciousness immediately after. Grendall tried a stamina spell, to no apparent effect. They continued on, eating their evening meal as they rode. Now, with the sun nearing the hill they had just descended, both of them had a bad feeling about this aelf, as if the darkness from the Darklands had followed them, casting an ominous shadow over them.

They made it across the valley, starting up the last hill before Westmoor, the sun well behind the hills they had crossed earlier, darkness surrounding them. Not wanting to attract any attention their way, they were wary of using their light. They went on in the darkness, relying on their moon vision to guide them. They could not see as far at night, seeing only as far as a human could during the day. During daylight, they could spot a deer almost four times the distance a human could.

Vorinelle mounted again when they crossed the apex of the hill, hurrying their horses. Westmoor was only a few hours away now. As they hurried down the hill, Vorinelle caught sight of a glimmer in the distance.

He whispered to Grendall. "There appears to be a fire below. Should we take a chance they have spare horses or just avoid them? They appear to be on the road; we will have to go far around to bypass them."

"I will go to the north with the horses." Grendall pointed to her left. "You creep up on them. See if you can identify them. If they seem friendly, give an owl's screech. If not, just go north and I will meet you a quarter hurs-marc due north of their position."

Vorinelle handed his reins to Grendall before leaving. He was quickly out of her sight, blending in with the tall grass and occasional bushes on the hilly terrain. Grendall dismounted, traveling as quickly and quietly as the terrain allowed.

Vorinelle slowly made his way down the hill until he could clearly see a campfire below. Around it stood a score of men with horses and two wagons. His heart lifted for a moment until he saw the emblem of a tower. They were knights, but not of the Silver Cross. While sure they would be safe, he was not so sure the knights would not take their prize and claim it themselves. In the end, the fatigue, cold, and pressing sense of doom decided the question. He hailed them from the darkness. A count of six later, they had formed into two rows, hailing him back.

"Who goes there at this hour? Come forward so we may know you, and whether or not you are peaceful."

"I am peaceful, good knights." Vorinelle walked slowly forward, keeping his hands out and forward in a sign of welcoming. "My name is Vorinelle. I am returning from a mission for Silver Cross Keep. I would welcome a warm fire, a hot meal and a safe place to rest."

"If you have papers from the Silver Cross, you will find friends here."

He noted a large, red-bearded man had come forward, sword drawn, searching the hill for him. He continued straight to the light. When the man found him, he met him a score of paces away from the other knights. Vorinelle reached slowly into his pouch, retrieving the scroll with the pact of service from the paladins. He handed it to the large man, who strolled slowly in front of him to the other waiting knights. He stopped as a thin, younger looking knight with a lantern walked up to the large man. They examined the document, the younger man handing it back to him and announcing, "Welcome, friends. I am Sir Barimor the Thorn, Banner Commander of the Knights of High Tower."

With the excitement over, Vorinelle informed Sir Barimor he had another friend to the north, asking permission to signal to her it was all clear. With Sir Barimor's nod, he let out a loud shriek which echoed off the hills above them. Within half an hour, Grendall appeared with the two horses, the knights gathering around them. A minute later, the camp was abuzz with men moving goods from one wagon to the next. For some reason they seemed quite agitated. They built a cot on the empty wagon for the unconscious Great Aelf. Soon, armed men were surrounding the two of them again, the Banner Commander towering over them with his sword drawn as well.

"Listen well, my popkins. You brought us a great aelf paladin, a member of the royal guard no less, unconscious and unresponsive. This will cause a lot of trouble with the aelf. So I am going to ask you a few questions. On my honor, if you give me the right answers, you can leave in peace. If not, then you best say your prayers, because you will not live to see the morning."

Vorinelle spoke, but the man put his sword to his throat. "You can speak when I ask the question." Seeing Vorinelle nod, he continued. "I don't want the entire story yet, but how did this aelf end up in this condition?"

Grendall spoke first. "We found him this way, Sir Barimor, in the Darklands."

"How did you find him?"

Grendall spoke again. "We were making a map of the Darklands for the Silver Cross paladins. We came across him, quite by happenstance."

"What happened to him?"

Grendall looked at Vorinelle, but he merely shrugged. "We do not know. He was in a spirit cage. We drained the enchantment from it, leaving him like this."

"Do you know who he is?"

"A Great Aelf is all we know." Vorinelle raised his hand to the sword and moved it aside. "He was naked when we found him."

"Why didn't you heal him?"

"We tried, with a stamina spell, but it didn't seem to help." Grendall said, getting over her shock. "We were hoping the paladins could revive him."

"Very well. You will live through the night. I will escort the Great Aelf to Gold Keep right away with a squad of knights. You will ride the rest of the way to Gold Keep at dawn with the rest of the banner. Try to leave, and we will kill you. Are we clear?"

"Yes, Sir Barimor." They replied in unison.

27<sup>th</sup> of Frendalo, Year 1124 AGW

Hills north of Westmoor

Grendall awoke with a hand pressed firmly over her mouth. It was pitch black within the tent. She struggled against the body lying against her until she heard Vorinelle whisper in her ear. "There's something happening in camp. Be as quiet as you can."

Vorinelle untied the tent ends, creeping outside. It was still pitch black. He led Grendall behind the tent, away from the camp. They heard the sounds of men fighting, loudly at first, slowly dying down until all was quiet. Vorinelle pulled Grendall behind him, the full moon illuminating everything. He led her to an outcropping of rocks about a hundred paces away, as they watched the camp.

"Over there," Vorinelle pointed to some brush, "Two of them, trying to flank us."

Grendall looked, but all she could see was the grass waving in the breeze around a thornbush.

"Do you have your fire blast?" Vorinelle asked her?

"Yes," she replied, not knowing where he was going with this.

"Do you see the small sourfruit tree over there?" pointing at a small, round bush to their left. "Prepare your spell. When I say, cast it there."

She prepared her spell, releasing it when he told her, "Now!" A ball of flame burst near the small bush, blazing for a few moments. Two figures were in the flames, one staggering and falling, the other diving to the ground to roll through the cool grass.

"I think you got one! Nice job. The other is creeping back to the right. See if you can-ughh!" Vorinelle staggered backwards, a small bolt protruding from his right shoulder.

Grendall pulled the bolt out, then grabbed a small vial from her pack, holding it to his lips. She could see the wound healing, but he lay there, still as death, looking at her. She let out a yelp as a bolt struck her in the arm. She reached over to remove it, her movements slowing until she just stared at it helplessly as she fell over. Paralyzed, she barely saw the dark figure approach. He pulled the bolt out before putting a black bag over her head. She could not move or see anything, but she could feel everything as he dragged her back to the camp. Her night clothes ripped and tore as he pulled her across the grass and small brush until he hoisted her up and threw her in the back of a wagon. She felt another body beneath her. After a short while, the wagon began moving, bumping and jostling her. She endured the pain for some time before she passed out.

28th of Frendalo, Year 1124 AGW

Just outside the Darklands

Grendall woke to water being thrown on her. She could move, but only slightly. The poison was wearing off. She struggled to move her arms to cover her naked body.

"Ah," someone said behind her. "You can move a little. That will make this much more fun." Grendall tried to turn her head to see, but before she could get her head turned, a small gong sounded, the voice continuing. "Let's begin."

A door opened, several footsteps following. Grendall watched a dozen Golden Aelf coming at her. She tried to scream, but no sound came out. The aelf came at her, half splitting off and going out of sight. Two of them pulled at her eyelids. Horrified, she had no choice but to watch as they used a razor to cut them away. Pulling chunks of her hair out, they forced her mouth open before slowly yanking her teeth out with tongs. After what seemed like hours of this, the actual torture began.

She tried to struggle, but the paralysis prevented her ability to fend off even the lightest pressure. Despite not being able to move, she could feel everything. It was a constant torrent of pain she could do nothing to relieve, not even scream. Her body instinctively tried to convulse, but it was reduced to nothing more than trembling.

"Catfly poison, dear. It paralyses the muscles, leaving the autonomous functions, like breathing, intact. And you still get to feel everything happening to you. Isn't it wonderful?" The woman giggled with glee like she had just told someone their Diromontous wish had come true.

Trying to speak back, even her cries of pain were silent. The voice continued to talk to her in a soothing, almost instructional manner.

"You know, it takes almost forty catflies to make one dose of the poison. As big as they are, you would think it would be fewer. They only develop the poison sacks when they are ready to breed, so you have only a couple of weeks to harvest them before they must lay their eggs. Normally, they must find a small creature, a mouse or a small bird, their poison will immobilize. Then they chew a hole, crawl under the skin, deposit their eggs and die. But it is OK, because they have fulfilled their purpose."

"The best part is the animal lives, immobile, but alive. Until a few hundred eggs hatch under their skin and the little larvae eat it alive from the inside out. The larvae will feast for two or three days, or until they devour the carcass. Then they burrow into the ground. A few days later they emerge as a new little swarm of catflies. They scavenge and grow for several months, when the entire cycle repeats itself. I should thank you two. You are going to do wonders for our breeding program. But now I must leave you to your torture." Grendall heard her footsteps leave and the door flap open and close. The torture continued.

They cut away strips of skin with a device much resembling a razor folded in half. Into the wounds, they poured powdery substances and liquids, each one more painful than the last. They used hammers on her hands and feet, breaking the bones. Then they twisted her arms and legs until the bones snapped. They continued grinding the bones against each other, bending the limbs until the bones cut through the flesh. After what seemed like hours of this, the elder aelf reappeared.

"Well, that was a productive day. Let's get you two cleaned up, shall we?"

She clapped her hands. The aelf dumped ice-cold water over them. Female aelf came with brushes, scrubbing their already scraped bodies. Afterwards, healers came. Grendall could feel the healing going through her. Throughout the next days and nights, her cuts and bruises disappeared, the gaps in her mouth filling in with new teeth. She slept and had dreams of being home in the Copper Woods, practicing her archery and spell craft and spending nights with Vorinelle.

෨෴

Just outside the Darklands

Grendall woke again to water being thrown on her. She could move more each day. The healing they had given her had revived her spirit as well. She turned to face the woman she knew was there. Sure enough, she heard the woman bang the gong.

"Ay!" Grendall tried to shout "wait," but it came out as barely a murmur.

"I'm sorry dear, did you need something?" the woman stood over her, looking straight down at her.

This was the first time Grendall had gotten a good look at her. She had dark hairs liberally mixed into the gray hairs, pulled back in a bun at the base of her neck, almost like the human paladins wore. Her eyes were golden. Grendall had never seen actual golden eyes before, but she had heard stories of the priests of the Gold Woods with golden eyes. Her skin was aged, looking like gold leaf behind a translucent glass. Deep lines etched her eyes and forehead, creasing her mouth, making her look like the old crones who sat outside the human cities begging for dolcots. Grendall tried to speak again.

"Leh tah.," Grendall forced out.

"Let's talk? My dear, whatever would you tell me? I already know everything you know. How you trespassed into the gasóga dorcha and stole one of my gineadóirs. Then you brought it to those cursed human knights who loaded it onto a cart and took it to the cursed paladins. There will be a storm dragon to pay after they figure out exactly what it is. Then we caught you and brought you here."

"En wa?" Grendall tried to ask.

"Why? Because I can. Because I have an entire tree of infantry here who wanted some entertainment. Because you embarrassed me by stealing the gineadóir. Because you make nice with the humans. Because you abandoned your own kind to be enslaved. But mostly, because it is fun, and I do so enjoy it." She banged the gong again, saying, "Let's begin,"

"Nooooo!" Grendall screamed, but soon she was screaming in pain as hands pulled her eyelids up and began cutting them away with a razor. Meanwhile, other hands began slicing strips of skin off her body once again.

## Outside the Darklands

Grendall woke again to water being thrown on her. Her body shook as the cold water hit her and she realized she could move. Once again, she turned to face the old aelf behind her.

"Stop this, please." Grendall pleaded, but the woman was having nothing to do with it.

In her grandmotherly voice, she simply laughed. "Now why would I do that, my dear. My soldiers have been expecting some live practice for their training. You wouldn't want me to disappoint them, would you?" She banged the gong, "Let's begin."

Grendall screamed, and the woman laughed again. Then she leaned over Grendall and taunted her. "Listen here, traitor. You should be happy I do not have the experts do this. They are much more cruel and much more practiced. These soldiers," she practically spit the word out, "are only practicing novice techniques. It is much worse when true artisans practice their craft. Then it is all about you, my pretty little plaything."

Many hours later, Grendall and Vorinelle lay near death, bleeding and oozing fluids from multiple wounds. The healers came, but the healing was different this time. Grendall could feel the healing energy coursing through her head, but it did not seem to penetrate to the rest of her body. Grendall didn't know how long she lay there. Her eyelids and teeth had grown back again, but the pain of moving or even breathing prevented any actual sleep. The only rest she and Vorinelle received was when they mercifully passed out. Still, she and Vorinelle hatched a plan.

৩৹৶

Just outside the Darklands

Grendall turned towards the movement of the tent flap opening. She had long realized her body was still mangled, but it seemed her head and neck were healed. She had never heard of healing so specific. She looked over to Vorinelle.

"We had to heal his body some, he would have died from his wounds otherwise. It won't do to have the main course spoil before it is ready to be served now, would it." Grendall turned to see the old aelf again.

Sneering, she turned and held Grendall's arms down. Now my sweet, since you have shown such fire, we will see if you can resist the swarm of cat flies we have for you. They will find your broken body and bite you. One won't paralyze you, but a hundred will. Then, while you can still feel it, they will eat their way into your body, burrowing under your skin to lay their eggs. Then they will die. But tomorrow, their eggs will hatch, and you will still be paralyzed, unable to stop them from devouring the rest of your flesh.

Pulling a device out from under the table, Baracom first placed one around the head of Vorinelle, and then turned back to Grendall. "This will protect your lovely face, so when they find your lifeless skeleton, your head will be perfectly preserved. Then the rest of your pathetic people will know not to come snooping where they have no business."

Placing it over Grendall's head, she signaled one of the aelf outside. "Release the cat flies." She turned once more to hold her face over Grendall. "It is not going to be a good day for you, my dear. But please know you are ensuring we will have thousands of doses of cat fly poison, creators bless you. Hear the buzzing? It is the sound of your end."

Grendall could indeed hear the buzzing. She had faded in and out of consciousness all night. When she was alert, she tried to move, and found her body so badly broken it hurt to even raise her fingers. However, she had endured the pain, and as the old aelf stood over her, she began the triggering motion for the spell she had cast hours earlier.

"Scaoileadh!" she screamed in pain as she touched her hand to the old aelf's side, ensuring it would strike true.

A bold of pure electricity ran out her hand and through the elderly Golden Aelf woman, continuing on to strike the two Golden Aelf guards who had accompanied her. The gray haired aelf writhed and jerked as the electricity ran through her. The two guards jerked a few times before falling stunned to the ground. Baracom Pattonos was made of sterner stuff though. "No little traitorous Copper Aelf is going to bring me down."

Sneering, she patted Grendall on the head. "It will take more than your weak power my sweet darling." Baracom stood to leave, but no sooner had she straightened, she let out a yelp, turning towards Vorinelle before freezing in place. Grendall saw the old aelf's eyes widen in horror at the realization she had just been stabbed with her own dagger. A dagger Vorinelle had managed to grab as she covered his head. A dagger covered in cat fly poison. Thousands of flies swarmed in. It would have been no problem for Baracom to have rushed out the tent and closed the flap behind her, but she could not move.

Grendall watched the aelf outside working frantically to repair the tent where the bolt of electricity had left it. Quickly fetching tarps and using pitch to seal the hasty patch, they were not paying attention to their leader. The only one who could have saved her was the aelf who released the flies, but instead of rushing in to help, she quickly went over and assisted the others with sealing the tent.

Vorinelle collapsed on the table, passed out. Grendall lasted several minutes more, feeling every bite of the flies, feeling them burrow down into her flesh as she struggled to rise to make her escape. She almost made it off the table before passing out herself. The flies, however, did not stop. Hours later, the last fly had eaten its way into one of the five bodies on the ground. None of the bodies were without oozing sores and lumps, making them completely unrecognizable, save the untouched heads of Grendall and Vorinelle.

The End

# SIR JAMES STONEHAND
by
Daniel E. Myers

28th of Frendalo, Year 1124 AGW

The morning sun was just rising as Sir Barimor rode up to the gate of Gold Keep. Riding the horses at a trot all night to get here, they lost one to exhaustion on the way. The surviving horses were lathered with foam. Stopping before the open gates, he hailed the guard.

"Knights of the Gold Keep, I am Sir Barimor of the Knights of High Tower. I humbly request passage into Gold Keep, and an audience with your Master and Commander."

Two paladins appeared almost immediately, riding out to meet the knights. One of them, riding a chestnut destrier with black stockings, came up beside them. "Hail and well met Sir Barimor. I am Sir James Stone Hand. Welcome to Gold Keep."

The knights dismounted, leading the horses under the front gate, through the gatehouse, and into a large courtyard. Around the stone walls were buildings which housed the blacksmiths and others who supported the order. Forty paces away was an impressive stone building, as tall as the walls, which housed the paladins stationed here. Sir Barimor knew three full spears of paladins could stay here. All around the keep were fully armored paladins going about their daily business.

"We have sent a message to Sir Erik the Scholar, our Master and Commander, with your request for an audience. He should reply soon. In the meantime, follow me to the great hall so you can get food and drink." Sir James waved at a squire, motioning him to come over. "Young Jeremy, take these horses, have them watered, fed and washed, then stable them in the north stables please. Park the wagon next to the stables for now."

"Right away, Sir James," the boy answered as he ran up to take the reins of the lead wagon horse.

"One moment please." Sir Barimor said as he raised his hand in a signal to stop. "Men, retrieve our cargo before they remove the wagon." The six men carefully pulled a makeshift cot from the back of the wagon and carried it over to their commander. Sir Barimor pulled the covers from the unconscious aelf and addressed Sir James. "Two aelf scouts hired by Silver Cross brought this aelf to us yesterday, along with quite a story."

Sir James looked at the aelf. "A Great Aelf. And you didn't heal him?"

"Yes. We tried anyway." Sir Barimor stated. "His body seems to be hale, but he does not wake up. He has been this way for three days now, two with the aelf and one with us."

Sir James removed his glove, holding his hand over the Great Aelf's forehead. "Deonaíonn biotáillí beannaithe do leigheas." A glow radiated from his hand to the Great Aelf, but his eyes remained closed.

"I do not feel so bad now," Sir Barimor exclaimed with a grin. "You understand why we must see your Master and Commander. Dinner can wait if it is all the same to you, Sir James."

"I do see. Thank you for bringing him here. I will leave as soon as we can get fresh horses for your wagon and bring him directly to Silver Cross Keep."

"The knights of Gold Keep are in your debt, Sir James."


30th of Frendalo, Year 1124 AGW

Sir James Stone Hand arrived at Silver Cross Keep just before sunset the next day. His men had ridden hard, particularly with a wagon in tow. The paladins caught sight of them once they raised their standard, sending a banner out to meet them.

"I must speak immediately with your Master and Commander." Sir James notified the paladin who met them as they rode to the gate.

A paladin a score of years older than Sir James replied to him. "I am afraid Sir Lolark the Luckless is at Foresight. He is attending the Palladium Council meeting there. I am Sir Benjamin The Bold. I am the Master of Arms, in charge while Sir Lolark is away."

"We are on our way to the Great Forest on a matter of utmost urgency. We ask you to supply us with fresh horses, food and water so we may continue our trip." Sir James would have liked to stop and rest himself, but something told him the Great Aelf would want their aelf back sooner rather than later. The fact none of the paladins could wake him concerned him greatly.

Sir Benjamin escorted him inside the keep, but insisted he explain the mission requiring they provide forty-eight horses, along with rations and water. Sir James revealed the aelf in the wagon. Sir Benjamin laid hands on him, also unable to raise him. Then he called for a high priest. Despite his best efforts, the priest could not rouse him either.

"This is quite perplexing." The priest commented. "If you travel to Tri-Keep, ask for Lord Sivle. He was my tutor. He may help where I cannot. He is also a friend of Sir Lolark and will resupply you as well."

Sir James thought for a moment. "We were not planning to stop at Tri-Keep, as we are hoping to ride straight through to the Freehold. However, if they might give us fresh horses, perhaps it would make sense to stop there. Are you sure they will assist us?"

Sir Benjamin spoke up. "I will send a letter with you on behalf of Sir Lolark. They will not deny you aid then. Be sure to get Lord Sivle's destriers for your mounts."

Within an hour, the paladins had restocked their food and water, replaced their warhorses, and hooked up another team to the wagon. Sir James was happy with their progress, going through the hills around the Great Chasm with a wagon was never easy. It was well-nigh impossible at night. Determined to make it to the Great Forest as soon as possible, he would not let a little thing like grendlaar infested hills deter him.

⳾⳾

31ˢᵗ of Frendalo, Year 1124 AGW

Three hursmarc south of Tri-keep

Sir James Stone Hand exhaled a great sigh of relief. After riding through the hills all night and most of the day, not seeing a single grendlaar, fortune smiled on them as they ran across a cart path running along the Great Chasm from Silver Cross Keep to Tri-Keep. Evidently there were regular shipments of food and other supplies which traveled the route. If the map were correct, they would approach Tri-Keep soon. Sure enough, as they came around a hill, they spied the tall tower of one of the three keeps. A small reddish colored dragon appeared overhead, circling several times before making its way lazily back towards the keep.

The paladins spurred their horses, riding the remaining hursmarcs to the keep at a light gallop, hoping to reach it before the sun set entirely. As they rode up, several wagons, followed by several animals, exited the gate, meandering their way out to the fence line. Sir James stayed on the wagon path to meet the wagons at the fence. Reaching the fence first, he had his paladins dismount and stand by their horses on the side of the road. Meanwhile he directed his men to pull their own wagon off to the side. As the outgoing wagons began going through the fence gate, he jumped at the sound of a voice next to him.

"I do hope you are not planning on taking my wagons, Sir knight."

Looking around, he noticed a diminutive man standing next to him. Sir James gave a curt bow. "Hail and well met. I am Sir James Stone Hand. I have no desire to take your wagons, or trouble you, good sir. I apologize if my men and I have inconvenienced you. Truthfully, I did not notice you as we rode up."

"I just arrived myself," the little man gave a brief bow as well. "I am Krom-gohlotsch. I have come to collect my wagons. And I am afraid there are no Na Oibrín for you to kill today. They are all safe in their homes."

"We have not come to kill anyone, much less the 'Nobrin' you speak of." Sir James found the little man's accent peculiar, wondering where he might be from. "We have found a Great Aelf paladin. Unable to rouse him, we are bringing him to the Great Forest to see if the aelf there can revive him."

The small man thought for a few moments. "The Mór-Oibrín helping the Tré Faðmlög? Curious. Weren't you just killing them the other day?"

Sir James was getting flustered. He was having trouble understanding this little man, and the man was talking nonsense as well. He suspected it was a language issue, however he was tired from traveling all night. "I have no idea who the 'Nobrin', or the 'Tria', whatever, are. And no, we have not been out killing anyone for some time now. But we have an injured aelf, and it is urgent to us to get him to where he can be healed. We were told the High Priest Sivle may be able to help, otherwise, we will take him to the Great Forest."

"Well, Sir James Stone Hand. I can see you are sincere in your desire to help this Tré Faðmlög, so I will provide you with some assistance. Clan Slayer is not here." The little man pointed toward the setting sun. "He has traveled back to the Mór-Oibrín city, but I will speed your journey." Then the little man disappeared and the sky turned dark as night.

Sir James looked up, completely mystified. Instead of the great plains and farmlands which had surrounded him, in front of him was a great forest of trees stretching as far as the eye could see. The wagon trail and fence were gone, replaced by a cobblestone road which led to the forest ahead. All the spare horses, including the ones for the wagon, were gone as well. Behind him, the plains stretched out. Not knowing what to do, he did the only sensible thing he could.

"Alright, men." he commanded. "Dismount and set up camp. First squad, you are on watch. Second squad, go scout the area and figure out where we are. Third squad, set up the tents and a picket. Fourth squad, get a fire and some dinner going. Everyone, stay on alert."

## Parts unknown

The third squad was on watch duty when they heard horses traveling down the cobblestone road. The squad leader quietly approached each tent, waking those inside. By the time the riders came in sight, the entire banner was armed, crouching in the tall grass, waiting to see who was approaching. Sir James stood with a torch in the middle of the road, to greet the travelers if they were friendly, giving them a suitable target if they were not.

The riders approached on lanky, painted horses. The horses wore light armor with green scale mail. Long, thin, leaf shaped plates hung down to protect the legs, with a chanfron shaped like a folded oak leaf covering the long, slender nose. A blue peytral with a silver tree in the center protected the chest. Four across, the riders made no effort to hide or even move quietly. The leader merely stopped his horse twenty paces from Sir James and called out.

"Hello friends!" Giving a small bow from his horse, "I am Sir Allier Duine Uasal, commander of the ninth banner of the fourteenth spear of the Army of the Great King Aedengus Duine Fionn. What brings you to sit at the door of the High Aelf kingdom."

Sir James could not believe it. Somehow, the little man had sent them over a day's ride away in the blink of an eye. He walked forward. "Form on me!"

Approaching the knight on the horse, he switched the torch to his sword hand, raising both to show he was unarmed. Striding forward, he answered the knight. "Hail and well met Sir Allier. I am Sir James Stone Hand, commander of the eighth banner of the sixth spear of the Order of the Gold Keep. We have come from Gold Keep with an injured paladin of the Great Aelf. He was retrieved from the Darklands."

With the mention of the Darklands, the aelf tensed. Sir Allier got down from his horse, approaching on foot. He walked to Sir James and reached out his arm. Sir James reached out and clasped wrists. "Sir Allier, please come see what we have and give me your council." Leading Sir Allier to the wagon on the side of the road, and the makeshift stretcher, he revealed the unconscious paladin. A hint of color had returned to his face. His breathing, though shallow, was regular and strong.

Sir Allier checked his eyes, which were light blue, noticing a pupil enlarged to where it nearly covered the iris. His heartbeat was strong, and Sir Allier could find no wounds or injuries which they had not healed. Unwrapping him entirely from the cloths they had bound him in, he checked his nether regions for indications of injury. Seeing none, he ordered his men to bring fresh cloths. They carefully wrapped him up again, repositioning him on the stretcher, adding the old cloths below him to provide additional padding.

After loading him back onto the wagon, Sir Allier spoke again. "I am sure his order will appreciate the care you have given him, Sir James. Since I am sure you would like to accompany him to the Great Forest, we will not take over his escort. However, we hope you will allow us to accompany you, to clear you through the checkpoints if nothing else."

Sir James thought about the offer, replying. "It would honor us to have your escort. Our horses traveled the better part of two days, however, and I am loathed to drive them any further this night. If we could leave in the morning and get fresh horses at the nearest garrison, we would like to ride straight through to the Great Forest."

"If it would please you, My Lord," Sir Allier said with a bow, "I can refresh your horses. They will make it to the Great Forest, where they will have to rest for a day, but we could leave now and arrive at one of their fortresses tomorrow."

With a noticeable sigh, Sir James agreed. "We would be in your debt, My Lord."

Sir Allier went to his pack, pulling out a sack with several small items which looked like adamons, only turquoise in color. Several of the aelf knights did the same, handing them to Sir James. "Feed these to your horses. They will make the trip at a strong pace." Sir James passed them out to his banner of knights, and they fed them to their war horses and the horses pulling the wagon. Within minutes, they were traveling along through the Great Woods.

ڡۤ

## Great Forest

Sir James was happy for the few hours of sleep he had gotten the evening before, but they had ridden at a fast trot the entire way through the Great Forest and fatigue was setting in. They had been up for the better part of two straight days riding over rough ground, despite the cart path. The few hours of sleep only made the body yearn for more. Still, they were done with their mission, and the day after tomorrow, they would all ride to the Freehold of Dragonsbane, spending a day or two there before heading back to Gold Keep.

They rode until they reached a grand temple in the middle of a clearing. Like most aelf temples, the trees themselves were purposefully grown and their massive trunks joined for the walls while intertwining branches made the ceilings. Sir Allier had sent riders ahead, so several priests were waiting for them when they arrived. As expected, the High Priest attempted to heal the paladin, but after the lack of success, they began preparations to bring him into the temple.

The priests carefully took the paladin from the cart and first stripped and washed him. An acolyte held a great silver bowl of water, while he continually chanted a heating incantation. They cleansed his entire body. Silver cups were used to pour the clean water over his hair, and after it was cleaned, they carefully brushed it, setting it back with wooden combs. When they finished cleaning him, they attached a holy symbol around his neck and wrapped him in pure white robes. They were careful to keep the holy symbol next to his skin. Next, ten acolytes and lower-ranking priests carried him into the temple. The High Priest approached Sir Allier, asking him, "Where did you find this paladin. Do you know who this is?"

Pointing at Sir James, Sir Allier replied. "It was this paladin, Sir James, who found him. We met them on the outskirts of the Great Forest. He thought you would be the best chance to revive him."

Turning to Sir James, the Priest then addressed him. "Sir James, I thank you for bringing our paladin back to us quickly. I fear they have used a dread magic on him. One which I do not fully understand, but I hope to find a counter to. Do you know who this paladin is?"

Sir James simply shook his head. "The knights who brought him to us detained the aelf who found him. We have only the map of where they found him and notes regarding the circumstances." He pulled two scrolls from his pouch, handing them to the priest.

The priest looked at the map, and seeing it was the Darklands, murmured silently to himself. Seeing there was no more information to be gleaned from them, he went inside the temple, followed by Sir James and Sir Allier. A great silver tree stood in the middle, its iridium branches reaching for the opening in the ceiling where the night sky was visible. Carefully cradling the paladin, they set him on the ground next to the tree, placing his hand on one of the silver roots. Then they began chanting.

The tree glowed slightly, illuminating the chamber. The paladin's body arched up in a convulsing spasm. Through the robes, the holy symbol glowed brightly. Slowly the robes darkened, first with sweat, then with blood, then with an ochre which turned them a bright orange. Still convulsing, the paladin writhed with the acolytes taking turns holding his hand against the tree, each one sweating and in obvious torment. The cleansing process was not meant to be shared. When it was,  anyone touching them shared the pain suffered by the supplicant.

The priests continued chanting even after the spasms stopped, and the eyelids of the unconscious aelf fluttered and opened. The paladin grabbed the root of the tree and lay there, in obvious pain, joining the priests in the chant, his robes clinging to his body. After another hour, he released the tree with a sigh, fading back into unconsciousness.

৯৫

## Great Forest

Sir James awoke to birds chittering in the surrounding trees. The sun was already a respectable distance above the horizon, but the trees did a fine job of keeping the clearing dark. Sir Rudolpho already had several fires burning and was brewing mace bean tea. Two quale boars were roasting on spits over two of the fires, and Sir James also saw what looked like venison next to the rotund cook.

Slowly rolling over, he looked over at his men. Most of them were still sleeping soundly, with a few looking like they were rousing from their dreams. He let his men sleep. He went over and got his tin cup out of his pack.

"Is the tea ready yet?" He asked his cook.

"Sir. Yes, Sir." Much spryer than his belly and his short stout body would let on, Sir Rudolpho sprung up from the ground, spun around and stood at attention, giving a smart salute with a big grin. It was not customary to salute in the field, certainly not when simply asked a question, but it was a regular joke between the two brothers.

Returning the mock salute, James reached over, scooping a ladle of steaming liquid into his cup. Smiling at his brother, he held the ladle out. Rudolpho immediately fetched a cup of his own, and they sat enjoying the cool morning together. The tea was not fully hot yet, but it cut the dampness from the forest air, and Sir James could feel the energy coming back into his weary body.

"Think dad got our gift yet?" James spoke quietly as not to wake the other men. "I was thinking of patrolling around the Chasm, maybe spending a night at the farm. We could stop by and catch the end of the Jubilee in Foresight too if we are quick."

Nodding slightly, Rudolpho answered thoughtfully. "Mom would sure love it. Sophia and Marella too. I'm not sure dad would be too happy at the surprise though. It disappointed him when I left, but he was outright angry when I came and got you, and you remember two years ago…"

Rudolpho left the last thought unsaid, both men exchanging frowns. Their last visit had been a disaster. Their father had stormed out as soon as they showed up, traveling to his brother's farm north of Tristheim. He didn't return for a month, leaving the girls and their mother to do the farming after James and Rudolpho left to return to the order. He wanted to make the point there would be no one to man the farm when he was gone, and therefore no one to take care of the women, and the boys got the message loud and clear.

"You've only got two years left on your commitment." James declared matter-of-factly. "Dad's not too old, and we can still take care of mom and the girls if something happens before then."

"I know, I know." Rudolpho replied. "But he still remembers his sister, and what happened to her when her husband died. He doesn't want that for mom and the girls. It isn't fair to you or me, but they are his responsibility, and I think when we left, he felt like he there wouldn't be anyone to take care of them if something happens to him."

James thought about it for a moment. "You were always more sensitive to everyone's feelings, I guess. If I had known he was going to be hurt so much by my leaving, I would have stayed."

Rubbing his little brother's hair, Rudolpho reassured him, "It's a good thing you didn't. I may have been more sensitive, but you always thought things through. When my commitment is over, I will go back and take over the farm. Maybe even find a wife. But you will probably command the entire order one day, little brother. This is what the Spirits made you for."

Their reverie was broken as Sir Reginald the Spiteful approached. "Is that venison?" Raising his voice, "Wake up everyone. We have venison for first-meal today!" He said the last with an enthusiasm which woke several of the men from their slumber.

The brothers looked at each other once more, then fell back into their knightly roles.

"Sir Reginald, if I had wanted to deprive the men of their much-deserved rest, I would have roused them myself this morning." Sir James stood at full height, forcing a dour expression onto his face. "Since you are full of exuberance and energy this morning, take three of the men you have awoken and go ask our host where to dig a latrine trench. And be quick, since we are going to make everyone wait to eat until you return."

Sir Reginald snapped to attention and threw up a perfect salute. "Yes, sir!" Then he quickly pulled three men from the group to help with his task.

Sir Reginald returned a few minutes later with a Great Aelf paladin and snapped off another salute and pointed off to his right. "Sir. The aelf have latrines set up a hundred paces in the woods there." Dropping his arm, he then waved it over to the paladin next to him. May I introduce Sir Vlaorelle Dragonheart, High Lord Commander of the Order of the Dragon. He would like to speak to you. Commander Vlaorelle, may I present Sir James Stone Hand, commander of the eighth banner of the sixth spear of the Order of the Gold Keep.

The aelf who stood before him looked to be ancient. His hair bore not a single tint of color and the olive skin the Great Aelf were noted for was albino pale. Yellow discolored the sclera of his left eye and his right eye bore a leather patch. But he stood tall, the focus of his good eye making it clear the mind behind it was still sharp.

"Hail, Commander Vlaorelle." Sir James raised his arm in salute. "To the Great King of Kings. May the Spirits protect him and his sons."

Raising his own arm, Sir Vlaorelle responded. "To the Kings of the Human Realms. May they forever live in brotherhood with the aelf."

The High Commander got right to business. "On behalf of the Great Aelf King, and the Order of the Dragon, we would like to commend your order for retrieving our fallen comrade. We are aware of the sacrifices made by the Order of the Silver Cross to investigate the Darklands and appreciate you bringing our comrade." Holding out a scroll, he continued. "The Great King of Kings would like to offer this commendation to the Order of the Silver Cross for their service to the Great King, along with a writ of one hundred havnots to offset the costs of these vital missions."

Sir James was speechless. The amount was unheard of for investigations, even ones which had gone on for as long as Silver Cross Keep had been searching the Darklands. But he thought he should say something before the silence became too awkward. Thinking back on what he had seen other commanders do, he seized on a similar experience his banner had been in when he was merely a mere squad leader. "I will pass this along to them directly. I believe they will be as taken aback as I am by your generosity."

Sir Vlaorelle continued. "For the paladins of Gold Keep, we offer each of you a commendation for service to the Order of the Dragon, and a writ for a thousand turots for returning our paladin to us."

"Humbly do we accept this commendation, High Commander. However, we must refuse the writ. To accept payment for merely doing our duty would bring dishonor and shame on our order."

It was Sir Vlaorelle's turn to be silent. To insist would be an insult to the men he was trying to honor. "Commander Stone Hand. Allow me to offer then, as a compromise, this writ as payment to the order for the hire of your banner for the time it guarded our comrade, and for bringing the maps and other information to us. We will also include a declaration your order is awarded the Dragon pennant, to be carried with your own banners wherever you see fit."

"Gold Keep would be honored above all words to receive such a declaration, but there is no need to reward us for doing what we have already sworn as our duty." Sir James' eyes pleaded with the High Commander to leave this issue lie.

But the High Commander persisted. "If it will help you retain their honor then, consider this a donation to the order, from a grateful recipient of its aid. But you will accept the writ. The King of Kings has commanded it."

Sir James bowed deeply. The discussion was over. He had refused the payment, and after the High Commander had offered again, refused. But now the High Commander had insisted. Honor had been upheld, and he graciously accepted the writ. "We are honored the King of Kings should show such great appreciation for our work. All of the human orders shall redouble our efforts to map the lands and determine a way to end the eternal night over them."

"Let me assure you, Sir James." Sir Vlaorelle spoke as he reached out his arm to Sir James. "You have just provided us with far more information than we have received from our own scouts and paladins. Like you, we have had difficulties with losing aelf in the darkness. We have scribes making copies of your maps and other information and we will return them to you shortly. In the meantime, please ask of us anything you may need."

As he reached out and clasped wrists with the aelf High Commander, Sir James answered him. "You have already honored us with your presence and your generosity. I am sure they are greater tasks awaiting you than greeting visiting paladins."

Reaching into his haversack, Sir Vlaorelle pulled another scroll out. "You again underestimate the service you have provided us today. We have provided fresh provisions in your wagon, and a fresh team of horses for it. I regret we cannot provide horses for you and your men, as our horses are not accustomed to bearing the weight of man and armor. I suspect your saddles would not sit well on them either. However, I have a writ for you to resupply at Tri-Keep on your way back to Gold Keep. It specifically requests Destriers, do not accept anything else."

Sir James tilted his head. "You are the second person to recommend their Destriers, Sir Vlaorelle. If I may ask, what is so special about them?"

Sir Vlaorelle shrugged. "Lord Sivle seems to be quite adept at breeding them. We only learned of them recently, as he is quite secretive about them. A banner of paladins of the Golden Chalice visited several months ago riding them. They are quite large and strong but also have surprising speed and endurance. For you humans with all your armor and accoutrements, they are perfect mounts. But he will not sell them to you if you do not ask for them specifically, and maybe not even then."

Sir James gave a small bow of his head. "Then we will be in your debt."

Sir James had not been planning on traveling through Tri-Keep, instead he was planning on resupplying at Dragonsbane. Since his wagon was full, he supposed he could ride the extra distance to Tri-Keep instead. It would mean skirting the Great Chasm on his way to Foresight. "Well," he thought. "I wanted to patrol, I guess this will be as good a path as any."

Sir Vlaorelle and Sir James clasped wrists again, and bowing to the younger human, Sir Vlaorelle turned sharply and left.

ꝶↄ

## Tri-Keep

Sir James grimaced at the thought of taking fresh horses from Tri-keep in trade for the ones he rode now. They had ridden their horses hard, knowing they would get fresh mounts from this Sivle fellow. As a result, several of their horses were foaming, all of them had thrown shoes, but they made the three-day journey in under two. They arrived hours before sunrise. He hoped he could rest his paladins while he exchanged the horses. Normally, it was a hard negotiation to get suitable mounts unless you were dealing with one of the other orders. Since Lord Sivle was not there to negotiate with, once Sir James announced his intentions, someone immediately summoned the stable master.

Sir Ecnirp the Purple was the stable master. Sir James tried to size him up before presenting the writ. A diminutive Great Aelf, short even for an aelf, Sir James could not decide if he was a bard or a jester, or just someone who really liked purple. He had purple riding trousers tucked inside black boots, with a lavender shirt and a riding jacket the same color and material as his trousers. Sir James dismounted. Deciding to intimidate the much smaller aelf, he stood at his full height, puffing out his chest as he handed the writ to the tiny keeper of the horses.

Sir Ecnirp didn't seem to notice. He took the writ and read it, then read it again. Looking up at Sir James. "Have your men dismount and unburden your horses, then set them in a line here." Without another word, he turned and left. Sir James was about to say something in response but could not think of anything. He had not expected this first negotiation to be so brief.

Sir James had his men do as the stable master requested. Shortly after his men had finished, the aelf returned with two stableboys. One had a large staff, the other a scroll and field desk. Sir Ecnirp had one stableboy hold the staff next to each of his paladins, and also across the horse. The aelf spoke in a strange language while observing the first stableboy, as the second stableboy scribbled furiously on a scroll. They finished in less than a score of minutes.

"Leave your gear where it is and return in four hours." The tiny aelf pointed at the three keeps, which were clearly visible. "There is a tavern and pleasure palace in the South Keep. There is an inn with good food and a temple in the North keep. If you need to replace any weapons or armor, the East Keep will provide it." The aelf and his two assistants picked up the desk and left.

Standing a little stupefied, Sir James turned to his brother, who just smiled at him. Turning to his men, Sir James raised his voice, "You heard the aelf." Pointing at the keeps in succession, "Ale and women in the south, food, beds and temple in the north, weapons and armor in the east. Return in four hours." A cheer went up among the men, then they went their separate ways. Looking at Rudolpho, Sir James pointed to the north. A hot meal and a drink sounded rather good right now.

They had time to visit all three keeps in the end. After eating and taking an hour-long nap, Rudolpho suggested they see what weapons the east keep had. Rudolpho had a strap on his scabbard which needed to be repaired. He had it tied securely, but it was always better to have a secure sword. The selection of weapons was spectacular, but the swords most of all. Sir James thought the armory at Gold Keep was well stocked, but the keep had an entire wall of swords which appeared to be enchanted. There were enough arms and armor here to outfit an army, which was odd considering there only appeared to be a spear of veteran soldiers running the keep.

Rather than repairing the strap, the armorer simply took the old scabbard and gave Sir Rudolpho a brand-new belt and scabbard, with a silver chape, throat and mid-hanger. The body appeared to be made of horn, with a dark gray luster. It was far nicer than the one he had just returned, and Sir Rudolpho cast a questioning glance up at the armorer. The man stood with his arms across his broad chest, biceps stretching his black tunic. His leather apron wrapped around his thick torso, tied in front.

"Not to your liking, sir?" the burly armorer asked.

"Not at all. I was wondering how much this is going to cost me. One of the simple leather ones would be fine."

The armorer uncrossed his arms, rubbing one hand across the stubble on his head as he explained. "The leather ones break too easily. We only issue those to soldiers or sell them to adventurers. Master Del Nileppez has instructed me to provide only metal or horn to the paladins. The horns are lighter, but you may have a metal one, in either silver or brass if you prefer."

"No!" Sir Rudolpho raised both hands. "This is magnificent."

"And what of you, sir?" the armorer directed his attention to Sir James. "Do you have need of anything from our shop?"

Sir James thought hard, but everything he had was new, or reasonably new. "Perhaps if you could repair this notch in my sword?" Pulling out his sword, there was a notch, ever so small, midway down the blade.

The armorer called out. "Vladimir, come here."

A young man, only twenty, came out of the back room. Dressed in long white robes, he looked like more of a temple acolyte than a blacksmith's apprentice. "Yes, Master Del Heinenkugel?"

"Take this back and cast a mending spell on it, please." The armorer carefully handed the sword to the young man. He pulled another from the rack, laying it on the counter. "If it pleases you, My Lord, take this instead. We will mend your sword, but you may prefer an enchanted one which will not chip so easily."

Sir James looked at the sword, noting it had the wavy pattern indicative of the Stein Virki smiths. They had learned a different technique to combine iridium with steel, reducing the amount of iridium required to enchant a sword. By the quality of the blade, Sir James could believe they enchanted it to prevent damage to the blade. Looking at the armorer, he set the sword back on the counter. "I cannot afford an enchanted sword, nor truthfully do I truly need one. I thank you for your generosity, Master Heinenkugel."

The armorer stroked his dark beard, thinking for a moment. He looked down at the sword, then back at Sir James. He spoke in a quiet voice. "To tell you the truth, Lord Sivle has his more advanced students do the enchanting as part of their training. We have scores of these right now. You would do me a small favor if you would accept it. Verily, I could supply both of you with one."

Still disbelieving his good fortune to have been directed here, Sir James picked up the sword, nodding a thanks to the armorer before sheathing it in his scabbard. It was narrower than his previous sword, but otherwise fit snugly and secure. Sir Rudolpho quickly exchanged his sword as well. Bowing deeply, Sir James thanked the armorer again as he and Sir Rudolpho left the large shop.

"Only one keep left to visit." Sir Rudolpho quipped as he finished securing his new scabbard. "We should send the men for a new sword too."

"Best not be greedy." Sir James replied. "I didn't want to take the diversion here just for horses, but I am glad we did. Now, let's go get a drink, shall we?"

The two men found most of the banner in the tavern. This early, just a few shady looking men conspired at a table in the back, looking at the paladins suspiciously. Sir James purchased a round of ale for the men. With almost half an hour to go, he sent two men to the pleasure palace to round up the rest of his men. After assembling the banner, he put them in formation and left to go get their new mounts.

Sir James prepared to negotiate hard for the horses. He was told to demand the destriers, and he intended to do so. When the horses arrived, he was at a loss. Fully a hand and a half taller than the plow horses he had grown up with, they still had the look of a war horse. The stableboys had gathered up each man's barding and saddle and accoutered the horses. When they brought him his horse, he noticed they had cleaned and polished his saddle and barding as well.

"We replaced your wagon horses and furnished you with some fresh supplies. We noticed you had no brandy, so we added a cask for you and your men." Sir Ecnirp stated crisply. "If you would leave your mark here, we will return the writ to the Great King." He held the scroll out to Sir James, as if he expected it to be signed. Frantically, Sir James thought to demand more, but Tri-keep had exceeded any requests he would have thought to make.

This Sivle was evidently one who honored the spirit, as well as the words of the Palladium Contract. Sir James wondered why they did not do more business here. He would keep this in mind if he traveled this way again. Signing the scroll, he handed it back to the small stable master, bowing to thank him, but the tiny purple clad fellow just turned and called back, "I assume this concludes our business. You are welcome to stay and rest at Tri-keep as long as you wish."

A cheer went up from the men, and they deserved the rest. However, Sir James wished to get moving towards Foresight. He compromised. "We will ride this afternoon to the town of Northfield to visit my parents, then ride the next day to Foresight to catch the end of Jubilee. Break off and report ready to ride in three hours." Another cheer, louder this time, and the men left the stables and raced back to the South Keep.

Town of Northfield, 20 hursmarc northeast of Foresight

Sir James rode his men late into the night, rousing them well after sunrise, even though he himself was up before dawn.  Rudolpho was up early as well and had begun cooking bacon over the fires he had built.  Scores of eggs sat in a basket next to him, likely brought out by their mother.  The smell of biscuits and fresh sweetbread wafted out from the house, and he was sure his mother would be bringing out an ample supply of both before the men rose.  He had helped milk the cows and then went with his father to look at the additions to the farm since they had left.

A new henhouse was over behind the house, along with a score of chickens pecking around.  Twice as many chicks were scratching at the seeds they threw on the ground.  His father mentioned they would mark one egg in four with blueash dye to make sure they didn't snatch it for firstmeal, and they would slowly fill the massive structure.  Over three scores could fit inside, and the small yard was fenced in with a latticework fencing designed to keep foxes and other small predators out.  The large buckhound which patrolled the farm would hopefully keep the larger predators away, but this close to the city, most of the larger animals were kept away due to the number of caravans and adventurers that traveled the road.

He also noticed the fence line seemed to travel quite a bit further out.  "You buy the Si Everson Place?" he asked his father.

"Only up to the creek. Griffith died this spring of lungrot and his son took over, but he can't handle the entire farm by himself.  Griffith always did have more land than sense.  But I guess he hoped to divide it among his sons.  Too bad he only had one." Smiling at his joke, Lloyd Si Billings thought silently on it for a moment, his smile reversing to a scowl.  But then he shook off the bad mood and continued. "We were always close to Griffith and Emily, so I agreed to farm it for five years and give them the wheat.  I also let them have Indigo for a week to stud their cows, and I get half the calves.  After five years, they can either take the land back, or I keep it if they decide they still can't handle it. Either way, they get help farming their land, and I get four more cows to breed each year."

James thought about the deal, and how it appeared to be heavily sided to the Si Eversons. But thinking it through, if the cows each had a calf, his father would get two more calves each year. Ten calves over the five years, or more assuming the Eversons kept some of the calves to raise and they started having calves. Father would certainly raise some of his calves, which meant he might have two score of birthing cattle by the time the deal was done. If the merchant was correct, his father would be able to sell havnots worth of cattle at the fairs. Even if he died, his mother would be able to pay someone to work the farm, maybe even sell it and retire in town.

After they finished the tour, he roused the men and they had their firstmeal. He thought of staying, but his sister Marella had been casting glances at one of the younger paladins, Sir Edward the Daring, and the two were caught kissing behind the house after breakfast. He would let Rudolpho handle that problem, he was not too sure of how Marella would take it if her younger brother commanded her suitor to cease and desist. But Rudolpho always had a way of convincing boys to leave the sisters alone without raising the ire of said young ladies.

Marella was past the age when she should already be wed and raising her own family. She had been engaged twice, only to have both men die; one from a bull goring him to death, and the other when he surprised a stone viper while bringing crops to Foresight. He took several days to die, and Sir James had thought if he had gone to Foresight instead of returning home, a cleric of sufficient strength could have cured him. As it was, the priest which led their small temple could only slow the effects of the poison. Rumors were Marella was cursed, and the offers to court her faded away. Perhaps with the dowry of a couple of cows, they might pick up again.

As they packed their horses a small crowd of townsfolk soon descended on the farm, and his men became busy demonstrating their martial talents as well as recruiting the young men and women who appeared to have an interest. A young orphan aptly named Hunter was among them. Only eleven, and small for his age, he showed a good deal of dexterity and actually did quite well with the crossbow, provided someone else loaded it. His sword skills were also impressive once they put a small short sword in his hands. He showed off tossing the sword in the air and catching it. He also showed a good deal of proficiency in several of the sword strokes they taught the young people who had an interest.

Completely enchanted with the paladins, he endeared himself to several with his earnestness. Some of his men, including Marella's Sir Edward, offered to squire him. Sir James' father noted that with no family, even if he never became a paladin, at least he would have good food and housing for a few years. Sir James thought about it all day, and finally in the afternoon allowed Sir Edward to squire him. All told they garnered four squires. He assigned them to the younger men, mainly to keep them busy and away from the town girls, including his sister. It was all for naught, as Marella was caught with Sir Frederick an hour later. Disgusted, Sir James ordered all of his men to mount up. They would eat immediately then ride hard to Foresight.

❧

## 20 hursmarc northeast of Foresight

Sir James had ridden the men hard, the destriers they had received proving up to the task. If they wanted to make it to Foresight by the last day of Jubilee, they would have to keep up the pace. Rudolpho was up early cooking bacon over the fires he had built. In the last week or so, their banner had transported a Great Aelf paladin from Gold Keep to the Great Forest, received fresh horses, and he had even obtained a new enchanted sword.

They had firstmeal and were making good time to Foresight. Rudolpho expected if they could keep up this pace, and every indication was the horses could, they would reach Foresight in the late afternoon. They were over halfway now, the city towers visible in the distance. His brother James even seemed to be chipper this morning, riding with his helm off, chatting with one of the new re-cruits they had picked up the night before, a young boy named Hunter. Hunter was excitedly pointing towards the southwest, Sir James was casually looking in that direction.

Sir James stiffened. replacing his helm. Rudolpho moved forward to see what was wrong, as he recognized the grim expression which consumed his brother's face. Rudolpho scanned the horizon, trying to see the source of the danger. Reaching his brother's side, he coughed softly to get his attention. Not wanting to alert the others, he nodded in the direction the boy was still pointing.

"The grass appears to be moving." Sir James whispered. "Looks like grendlaar, and a lot of them."

Sir Rudolpho drew his breath in sharply. Scanning the horizon, he could not see what his brother was referring to. In the distance, the grass waved in the wind, just like any other day. Then he noticed it. There was a definite edge where the grass was moving. In front, the grass was still, but as soon as it hit the line, it was waving back and forth. And the line was moving towards Foresight. He traced the outline, and his heart came up into his throat. From front to back, it was hundreds of paces long stretched past the horizon. There would be tens of thousands of horrid little monsters in a pack that large.

"There must be thousands of them." Rudolpho told his brother quietly.

"A score or more, I would guess. I cannot tell where the far side ends though." James raised his fist in the air, signaling his men to stop.

The paladins gathered around to discuss their options. Basically, there were three. Ride and attack the hoard immediately, sending a rider to Foresight to warn them while the rest delayed them. Or they could all ride for Foresight to assist in the city's defense. The third option would be to ride back to Tri-Keep to send messengers to all the nearby cities to send aid. No one voted to ride back to Tri-Keep, while only eight voted to ride to Foresight. He counted thir-teen hands raised to ride to intercept the hoard. Sir James questioned the math until he saw Hunter's hand raised high to intercept the grendlaar army.

"It is decided, then." He pulled Hunter aside and told him to get the other recruits onto the wagon. "Escort the squires-to-be due west to circle around the city and wait. When the battle is over, come find me." While Hunter protested initially, he acquiesced once they brought the other youths forward, putting them under his charge. Sir James took Hunter's hand in his and told him. "You are responsible for keeping them alive now."

The paladins escorted the wagon west for half a hursmarc and then turned Southwest. What he thought a score of paladins would do against a thousand score of grendlaar, he did not know. Outnumbered by even the grackles ten to one, such was the fate of a paladin. They were honor bound to defend those in need, despite the odds. Lining up the men and women under him in two ranks, they began a steady gallop. They would have to ride hard to catch the grendlaar before they got to Foresight.

It soon became clear they would not catch them. The grendlaar moved too fast. In a few hours, the grendlaar would cross the Dark Water River, and Sir James and his men would still be over a hursmarc away.

With nothing left to do, Sir James had his men raise red warning pennants on their lances and ride towards the city. His horses were panting when they saw the city gates, still several hursmarc away. He had his trumpeter sound his trumpet with the two short blasts followed by the long high note signaling an attack. He heard no trumpet in reply. They rode another hursmarc and tried again. Torches illuminated the castle walls, a trumpet replying. Slowing his men to a trot, he hoped to reach the bridge across the Dark water before the Grendlaar began their attack.

One hursmarc east of Foresight

Graelshnar's Mtumwa had managed to approach within a hursmarc before he heard the horns warning them their attack was no longer a surprise.

The aelf Aduialon had lent him to eliminate the human scouts did their jobs well. Sooner or later they were bound to be detected, and he was happy they had made it this close. In just over a quarter of an hour, they would be on the humans, and his people would swarm them and kill them and be killed in return. He looked northward and could see the telltale dust cloud Inkunzi and his cohort were stirring up as they advanced as well. Almost twice as far from the city as he was, they were making up the time lost from crossing the river.

In the city, more and more horns were beginning to sound. Slowly, men were filling up the top of the city wall. Cursed archers and mages would be lining it shortly. But the people did not fear human arrows. By the time the archers had loosed a flight and nocked another, his people would have moved a hundred paces. Once they were in among the warriors, the archer fire would slow down, and his Mabwana wa Mtumwa would be targeted. He would be targeted as well, the light scale hauberk he wore providing scarce protection.

But his Mtumwa were tough. It would take more than an arrow wound to stop them. After they pulled the arrow out, they would have another weapon to attack with. As they neared the city, they could see the humans forming a long line of defense. A quarter hursmarc of open field stood between the city and the nearest tree, and even those were scarce. For some reason, the warriors were in front of the city walls, instead of using them as an impenetrable extension of their line. A few minutes later, he understood why.

A large barn with animals being led out was behind the warriors. A long line of people and carts, as well as animals of all sorts, was stretched out in tendrils from the main city gates. Disordered and slowing down the ones behind in their rush to get to safety, the stupid humans were stopped by the very guards which should be coming out to fight him. His Mtumwa would reach the line of warriors long before those wagons were inside. And his Mtumwa would slaughter them, like the metal men slaughtered the Mtumwa farmers and tradesmen whenever they found them.

Less than a thousand paces away the first arrows began falling among his Mtumwa. Most drove harmlessly into the ground, to be picked up and wielded by one of his charging warriors. One drove into the skull of a soldier, dropping her. Another, likely her mate, cradled her briefly and pulled the arrow out before he began his charge again. Hundreds of arrows fell, and a score of his warriors lay on the ground to be trampled by the hoard behind. But he had half a jeshi of warriors, his losses so far were lighter than he could have hoped for.

A hundred paces from the now solidified line of metal men he slowed his charge to allow his Mtumwa to pack themselves in a dense mass. In this way they could overwhelm the shields of the humans and pull them down with sheer weight of numbers. A metal man was vulnerable when lying on the ground. Spears could prod their weak points, and even the metal armor could be punctured if enough spears struck it. His soldiers had reached a solid mass, and he raised his hand to give the order to charge.

The soldiers did a strange thing. The lines separated, men moving back and forward and to the side, leaving great holes in their line. Then cursed metal men on their horses charged through the gaps. Stopping his charge, he gave the order to set their spears. As they had trained, his mtumwa stopped where they were and set their spears. They would not stop the horses, but they would slow them down. Sooner or later a spear would find a weak spot, or tear off a piece of the metal, and then the horse and rider would fall.

Over to his left, a herd of centaurs clad in metal were charging around the edge of the line of warriors. Hundreds of them, all armed with spears and swords and lances. He remembered when he was young and had fought along-side the centaur during their war with the humans. Now they had befriended their vanquishers and fought alongside them. Graelshnar watched proudly as one of his induna turned her umndeni to face this new threat. Several other umndenii followed suit, until the entire left side of his line was turned. Then the horsemen and centaurs hit his lines.

The End

(Find out what happens with Sir James in Attack on Foresight., Book II of The Knights' Trials.)